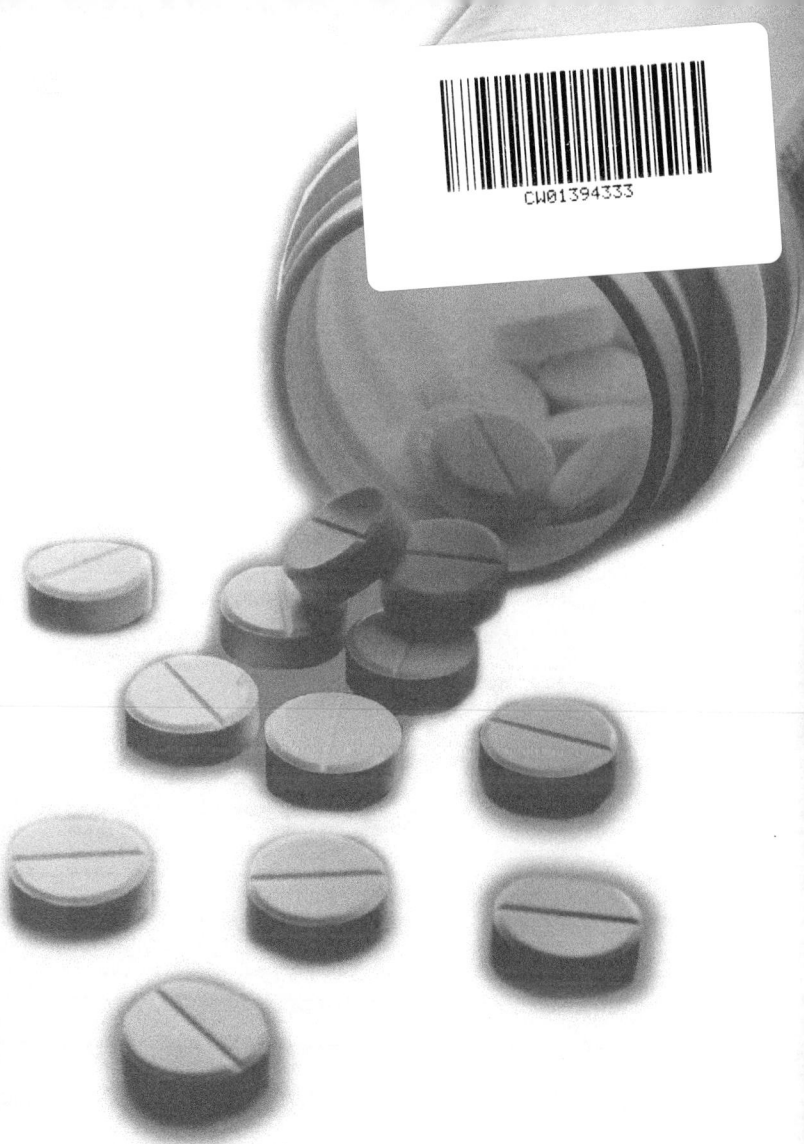

MERCY

OR MERCENARY?

SHEILA PARKER

Matador
9 Priory Business Park,
Wistow Road, Kibworth Beauchamp,
Leicestershire. LE8 0RX
Tel: 0116 279 2299
Email: books@troubador.co.uk
Web: www.troubador.co.uk/matador
Twitter: @matadorbooks

ISBN 978 1789013 528

British Library Cataloguing in Publication Data.
A catalogue record for this book is available from the British Library.

Printed and bound by CPI Group (UK) Ltd, Croydon, CR0 4YY
Typeset in 12pt Adobe Garamond Pro by Troubador Publishing Ltd, Leicester, UK

Matador is an imprint of Troubador Publishing Ltd

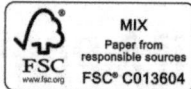

With thanks to Gill, Pat and Davina
for all their support and encouragement.

1

'What's the matter? Is it Ralph?' demanded Isabel, and pushing Joanna aside, she ran up the stairs.

Ralph McGuire, her husband who had been suffering from Alzheimer's for the last three years and whose condition was deteriorating, was lying on his back, his eyes open and staring, his hands resting on the turned-down duvet.

Three buttons of his pyjama top were undone while two pillows (used when he sat up) were on the floor.

Running forward, Isabel felt his throat, then his wrist and rushing from the room muttered, 'I must phone the doctor. There's no pulse or heartbeat.' And as Joanna, still speechless, followed her downstairs, Isabel asked, 'What happened?'

'I don't know. I wasn't there.'

'What do you mean; where were you?' And as Joanna mumbled, Isabel persisted: 'Why weren't you with him? Why did you leave Ralph?'

'A man called to see him, said he was a friend. He was very insistent.'

Joanna stared as Isabel stated it was an emergency, that the doctor should come at once and then demanded, 'Who was this man? How long did he stay?'

'Ten minutes, maybe a little longer. When he left, he told me not to disturb Uncle, he wanted to have a rest,' Joanna faltered. 'At first, I wasn't worried. I had spoken to Uncle earlier and then just sat with him. He seemed rather sleepy, so I was annoyed when this person arrived and that he was so persistent. I waited for about ten minutes after he'd gone.'

Joanna jumped as the front door, which was still ajar, was pushed open and a young man entered, greeted them briefly and ran upstairs. Isabel was immediately behind him, but on reaching the top of the stairs she turned round. 'Where's Elspeth?'

'It's such a lovely afternoon I suggested she should go for a walk. She'll probably be back–'

Again, Joanna broke off as Elspeth came through the still-open front door. 'I saw the doctor's car. What's happened?'

Elspeth felt that the minutes she waited on the landing outside Ralph's room were endless and was sure that Joanna, who was now nervously wringing her hands and shifting her weight from one foot to the other, felt the same.

The doctor's voice was only a murmur, then he

and Isabel, looking pale and distressed, emerged. Dr Beresford glanced at Elspeth. 'I'm sorry, my dear. Ralph was dead when I arrived. I suggest some hot, strong tea and, as I'll be here for some time, I'd like a cup,' then, looking at Isabel, 'may I use the phone in the study?'

'Of course.'

'Uncle Ralph's dead so why is the doctor still here, who's he phoning?' asked Joanna a few minutes later as they sat around the kitchen table.

'The police,' said Dr Beresford as he entered the kitchen. 'I'm not very happy about the cause of death, that there are no tablets left in the bottle in the bathroom cabinet.' The doctor nodded his thanks, pulled out a chair and sat down, then picked up a mug of tea, drank some and, glancing at Isabel, repeated, 'I can't understand why the bottle that contained his tablets is empty. I'm afraid that this will necessitate a visit from the police.' He then turned to Joanna. 'As you were the only person in the house when this stranger called, they'll want to question you.'

'I didn't do anything!' exclaimed Joanna. 'I only sat with Uncle Ralph. I didn't go into the bathroom or near the cabinet where his tablets are kept; he was fine then, just confused.' The ringing of the doorbell startled them all, but it was Joanna who burst into tears.

2

'Was your uncle expecting anyone?' enquired Inspector Kershaw after he had learnt that the caller had given no name and had worn a wide-brimmed hat, making it impossible for Joanna to see his face. Although it wasn't cold, he had worn a thick overcoat and scarf, and his voice had been muffled.

'No. I told Uncle Ralph last week that I'd be coming today, but when he saw me he was surprised. I doubt that he remembered.'

In reply to the inspector's further questions, Joanna repeated that she obviously didn't know if the caller had removed his hat, scarf or coat and that on leaving he said that her uncle didn't wish to be disturbed. Nevertheless, about ten minutes later, she had gone upstairs, pushed the door open and, to her amazement, had found Uncle Ralph lying flat on his back as the inspector had seen for himself. 'I didn't touch him, I couldn't. I know it sounds dreadful. I'm twenty-seven and have a responsible job, but I was too frightened. I ran out onto the landing, and although

4

it wasn't very long, I was so relieved when Isabel returned.'

'Did anyone else go into your uncle's room?'

'No. We were the only people in the house.'

'Until the so-called visitor arrived,' persisted Kershaw.

'He was definitely here.' Joanna glared at the Inspector, her dark brown eyes emphasising her pallor.

'We've only your word for that.'

'He brushed past me, didn't give me a chance to speak or protest and went straight upstairs. Someone must have seen him.'

'Was there a car parked outside?'

'I don't know. Maybe one of the neighbours saw him arrive.'

'That's possible; it is Saturday.' Kershaw told Detective Sergeant Small, who had been taking notes, to arrange for the neighbours to be questioned and turned back to Joanna. 'You've referred to this visitor as a man but could it have been a woman?'

'It's possible.' Joanna frowned. 'Because the hat was pulled right down, the scarf covered the mouth and nose so I couldn't see much of their face.'

'Did you notice the colour of their eyes, shape of their eyebrows or nose?' persisted Kershaw.

'No. As I've already told you, the hat had a very wide brim.'

'Thank you, Miss McGuire. You've been very helpful.'

'How are you feeling, Mrs McGuire?' enquired Inspector Kershaw.

'I still can't believe Ralph's dead.' Isabel sank into a shabby armchair and gazed at the chief inspector, grateful for his consideration and empathy. Learning his rank , she had expected an older man but guessed that this tall, well-built man wearing a smart suit was in his mid-forties. She had also noticed that the sergeant, who was copiously taking notes, had thick wavy hair, a smooth complexion and a pleasant manner. 'We knew he was suffering from Alzheimer's, that he was deteriorating but…' Isabel hesitated and, looking at the inspector who was sitting opposite her, asked, 'How did he die?'

'We don't know yet but as you already know, the bottle containing his tablets is empty.' Kershaw noted her pallor and said gently, 'I realise this is all very upsetting and you don't have to tell me now, but have you any idea how many tablets were left?' On learning that there were approximately fifteen left, he wondered what had been used to crush these before they were added to Ralph's drink, considered that the perpetrator had acted very quickly and, without elaborating on this, he resumed, 'There'll have to be a post-mortem, but now I'd like to ask you a few questions.'

Isabel nodded when Kershaw learnt that Ralph always refused to see any unexpected callers. 'I'm amazed that anyone should be wearing a heavy overcoat on such a warm day. It must have been someone who didn't want to be recognised.' She then stated that Ralph only tolerated Joanna and, since his return, Duncan Sinclair, a colleague who was now helping her with the biography of Leo Adare.

'He occasionally saw Hugo.' Isabel explained that Hugo Forrester was the managing director of the company who published the biographies and had become a personal friend. Although he knew that Ralph was deteriorating, Hugo had been shocked to hear of Ralph's death. He had offered to drive down to Bristol immediately but agreed that, at the present time, there was nothing he could do, and offered to tell Leo Adare.

'I understand that Elspeth was also out?'

'Yes. Apparently, Joanna suggested that as it was such a lovely afternoon Elspeth should have some fresh air.'

'So neither of you saw this unexpected visitor?'

'No, and I certainly don't know any of Ralph's friends, acquaintances or colleagues who own a wide-brimmed hat. Perhaps Elspeth can help you.'

Inspector Kershaw knew that Elspeth and Isabel had been close friends since their schooldays and were the same age but considered that Elspeth, with her gleaming chestnut curls, flawless complexion and wearing a cream linen suit, looked considerably younger.

He was surprised that she had lived in the old family house with her brother for so long, remaining there after he had married and had learnt that she was a proofreader for a well-known publishing company.

But before he could speak, Elspeth said, 'I wish I hadn't gone out this afternoon. I certainly wouldn't have let someone we don't know see Ralph. Joanna shouldn't…'

'I don't think you can blame her, Miss McGuire. Apparently, this person just pushed past her. However, although you didn't see him, can you recall anyone who wears an Austrian-style winter coat, fedora and scarf, visiting your brother? And I don't mean recently.'

Elspeth looked thoughtful then shook her head. 'No, but it's possible he may have called on occasions when I was out and, as for his hat and scarf, he could have disposed of these.'

'Good thinking.' Kershaw glanced at his sergeant. 'Make a note that the neighbouring gardens and litter bins are checked.' Then turning back to Elspeth, 'Apart from Joanna, who were your brother's regular visitors?'

'There weren't any. He didn't want to see anyone, even Hugo Forrester who, as you already know, is the managing director of Ralph's publishing company, and also a friend.'

'What about Leo Adare?'

Again, Elspeth shook her head. 'Ralph hasn't seen him since they first discussed the biography. At the time, Leo agreed to give Isabel the names of friends or theatrical colleagues, and any assistance she required. Isabel has been doing all the necessary research over the past eight years and she's done most of the actual writing for the last four. Ralph, of course, received all the praise. The Alzheimer's started three years ago, but in the last few weeks his condition has deteriorated considerably. It's no wonder Isabel looks so tired. Fortunately, Duncan Sinclair has returned to help with the research.'

Kershaw glanced at the list of people who had been in the house during the morning and early afternoon, didn't see anyone of that name and asked, 'Why isn't Sinclair listed here?'

'He's away interviewing some of Adare's colleagues.'

Having learnt that Duncan had recently returned from Guernsey, quickly becoming absorbed in Adare's biography and the research, Kershaw asked 'I would like to see Mr Sinclair when he returns. Do you know when that is?'

'No. I'm sorry, I can't tell you that.'

'Ralph's dead!' exclaimed Duncan early that evening when he phoned, then after Isabel's brief explanation and regardless of the fact that he had more appointments on Monday, he asked, 'Would you like me to come back now?'

Isabel hesitated and then said, 'No thanks. You've

9

interviews scheduled, so it's best that you carry on as arranged.'

'I don't like the thought of the police pestering you and Elspeth with questions,' said Duncan.

'Hopefully, there won't be any more.' Isabel paused and then said quickly, 'I suppose that depends on the post-mortem.'

'Don't worry; I'm sure there's nothing untoward.'

Then, as the thought occurred to him, Duncan asked, 'Does Hugo know, and what about Joanna?'

'She was here at the time and I spoke to Hugo earlier.' Isabel recounted Hugo's offer to inform Leo Adare and his insistence that they should continue with the biography.

'You surely didn't expect him to say anything else, did you? You've always done most of the work and let Ralph take all the credit!' Duncan ignored Isabel's protests. 'Although I was out of the country most of the time, I know what's been happening. I must say that I'm disappointed that Hugo, who knew you were coping with the research and the writing, didn't ensure that you received due praise.'

'Now you're being ridiculous,' said Isabel and, as requested, handed the phone to Elspeth.

'What happens after the post-mortem?' asked Joanna later as they sat around the kitchen table eating lasagne and salad. It was after she had been questioned by Inspector Kershaw that Joanna had become hysterical, and Dr Beresford, who was still in the house, had been concerned about her. Isabel and Elspeth had quickly suggested that as Joanna lived alone she should spend the weekend with them. Joanna had quickly accepted this invitation and looking at them, now waited for an answer.

The two friends exchanged a warning glance and it was Elspeth who spoke. 'I shouldn't think or worry about that. One way or the other, we're going to be busy so, if and when you have any spare time, we'll be pleased with your help.'

'Work,' echoed Joanna. 'I don't know that I'll feel up to it on Monday.'

Joanna was head receptionist at a large hotel near the centre of Bristol and, suppressing her exasperation, Isabel said, 'I think you should. You often tell us how busy you are but that you enjoy hotel life.'

Joanna nodded. 'You're right. It's not as though Ralph was my father.'

Then glancing at Isabel, 'I know one shouldn't speak ill of the dead but, according to Mother, he was very unpleasant, even as a child. Although younger, he used to bully her into doing all sorts of things for him, helping with and even doing his homework.'

'So he hasn't changed in that respect,' said Isabel, stacking the plates and standing up. Aware that Joanna was gazing at her curiously, Isabel continued,

'Obviously, I'd known Ralph for years, ever since Elspeth and I became friends, and I was amazed that he should choose me as his research assistant. It's always been very interesting, even when he was doing the television series and he could see that I was willing to help him.'

'To the extent that you gave up your job as English teacher at Redmaids which, although I didn't say so at the time, I thought was a great pity. You were popular and respected by the other teachers, and your pupils.'

Elspeth ignored Isabel's protests and resumed, 'Ralph always knew that you were very thorough and methodical but never admitted that you were also highly intelligent.'

'Now you're talking rubbish,' but in spite of herself Isabel smiled. 'I was even more surprised when he proposed. At the time I was doing so much writing of the biographies that I didn't bother about clothes or my appearance, but that didn't matter to him.'

'And now you can carry on, at your own pace.'

3

That night, as she lay in bed, Isabel still felt guilty that she was unable to shed any tears over Ralph's death. She realised that Joanna was still shocked at the manner of his death, particularly as she had been in the house at the time, the arrival of the inspector, and his subsequent questions.

Elspeth had been marvellous, agreed that Joanna should stay with them and, as always, had been a tower of strength. Isabel recalled Duncan's offer to cancel his arranged interviews and return but still felt that, at the present time, there was little one could do.

It was good to know that Duncan was back in England and, turning over, she recalled their unexpected encounter in the library and the events that had occurred in the following weeks...

Isabel stood on tiptoe and reached for a biography on an upper shelf, but the dust jacket slipped from her grasp, then a hand covered hers and a voice, somehow familiar, breathed, 'Can I help?'

Unable to release her grip, Isabel noticed that the hand was soft-skinned, tanned and the nails manicured. The pressure was maintained, causing a shiver of fear, or was it anticipated delight as she lowered her arm, thus regaining her normal height then, turning round, she found herself looking into a pair of twinkling blue eyes and stammered, 'Can… can I have my hand back, please?'

'In a moment.' The voice was gentle, persuasive and reminded her of someone she had known years ago, then its owner continued, 'It's a very hard-working hand, like its owner who I notice has changed considerably.'

Isabel was immediately aware that her hair was lank and badly needed cutting, while her dress was crumpled, and that her face, devoid of any make-up, even lipstick, had not received any care or attention for a long time. Embarrassed and conscious of his intent gaze, Isabel asked, 'Duncan, is it really you?'

'Yes. Unfortunately, it's been a long time – my fault, I know – since we last saw each other. We did meet Monday evening but only for a few moments. Ralph, your husband, was about to reintroduce us when his memory failed.'

Isabel nodded, remembering the occasion: a drinks party given by a well-known judge whose biography Ralph had written. Aware that her heart was pounding and her pulse racing, Isabel remembered that she had felt exactly the same when she first met Duncan, many years ago, when she was at university. She had met a number of men in the intervening years, but Duncan was the only person to have that effect, and he had still been in her thoughts when she agreed to marry Ralph thirteen years ago. Dismissing these thoughts, she said, 'Duncan! Was that really you on Monday? You looked so different.'

Immediately, the lop-sided grin that she had known so well appeared. 'Yes. I'm the same Duncan Sinclair whom you knew years ago. It's surprising what shoulder-length hair, a beard and scruffy clothes does to a person. I'd come straight from Gatwick. Didn't your husband tell you about me and his plans? However, as we'll be spending a lot of time together, I'm quite prepared to grow both again, if you wish.'

'What!' Isabel wriggled her fingers. Duncan had almost crushed them, but before she could continue, Mr Elliott, the head librarian, was approaching.

'Good afternoon, Mrs McGuire. How are you? And Mr Sinclair, it's good to see you again. I understand you'll be staying,' and his gaze incorporating Isabel, 'and working with Mrs McGuire.'

'I...' Isabel opened her mouth, gazing at the librarian and then Duncan. 'What's going on? Why...?'

'Didn't Ralph tell you?' asked Duncan while the librarian apologised, 'I'm sorry, Mrs McGuire. I thought you knew; that Mr McGuire had consulted you before making these arrangements.'

'What arrangements?' Isabel frowned, rubbing her brow. 'This is very confusing. There are days when Ralph can hardly communicate, let alone make arrangements.'

'I think we all need a cup of tea or coffee,' said Duncan and glancing at the librarian, 'will you join us? Help me explain what, unbeknown to Isabel, Ralph has arranged.'

Ten minutes later, Isabel sighed, helped herself to an éclair and said thoughtfully, 'So Ralph spoke to you both about this six weeks ago?'

'Yes, and at the time he was very lucid. He told me that he had just spoken to Mr Sinclair before he phoned me, and I agreed that I would help Duncan in every possible way, arrange for further reference books or whatever else you required.'

Mr Elliott refilled their cups and resumed. 'I didn't mention this conversation when you came in the next day. I presumed the matter had been discussed and agreed.'

'That's about the time Ralph's memory started to fail. He'd get so cross, even angry.' Isabel omitted to say that Ralph blamed her on these occasions and continued, 'Then he started getting confused, mixed-up, not knowing if I was Elspeth or even Joanna, his niece.

'This morning, he was worse.' Isabel did not say that Ralph had been unable to speak and when he did, his words were unintelligible.

'What time does the nurse come on duty?' enquired Duncan.

'Nurse!' echoed Isabel. 'He won't tolerate one except to help with the real necessities.'

'But even with Elspeth's help you can't surely cope,' protested Duncan. 'I must say I thought Ralph looked quite well on Monday. Although he only uttered a few words, he seemed confident Leo's biography would be finished on time.'

'I'm doing my best but it's very difficult. There aren't enough hours in the day.'

The two men exchanged glances and Duncan was sure the librarian shared his thoughts, that Ralph was probably an awkward and demanding patient. Then turning to Isabel he suggested that, although it had been arranged for him to start the following week, he would accompany her home and pick up the draft and last chapter that had been completed. He would study these and the notes for the remaining chapters that evening and start in the morning. Signalling for the bill, Duncan continued, 'You can tell me about it and what you think of Leo Adare on the way.'

The librarian stood up and looked at Isabel with concern. 'I'm glad Mr Sinclair is here to help you with this biography. However, do try and persuade Ralph that he should have a nurse, even for a few hours a day.'

It was as they approached the top of Park Street that Duncan stopped suddenly. 'I don't want to hurt your feelings, but I honestly didn't recognise you on Monday. I know it's a long time since we were both at university, but what's happened to you? Have you been ill?'

'No.' Isabel looked up at Duncan, enjoying the unusual warmth of the early April sun on her shoulders.

'I realise I look a mess. I shouldn't have let it happen. It's just that I've been so busy.'

Duncan nodded. 'As I said before, you've been working too hard. I remember that you were always very capable, but I'm surprised Elspeth hasn't commented.'

'She has.' Isabel pushed a strand of hair behind her ear. 'However, Ralph insisted that I acquire the information he needed…' Isabel paused. 'You don't need to hear all this. Even though you've been away, latterly in Guernsey, you've known Ralph for a long time, how absorbed he becomes and that nothing else matters. Anyhow, I must get back or he'll say I spend too long in the library.'

They had now reached the Victoria Rooms and as they turned left Isabel began to walk quickly and it was with considerable restraint that Duncan refrained from saying, 'Surely he doesn't time you?' Instead, he said, 'We're almost there but don't worry about me. Go up and tell him you met me in the library. I'll spend a few minutes in the study and then come upstairs.'

The sight of Elspeth standing at the top of the stairs, almost outside Ralph's room, indicated that he was being awkward, and Isabel hurried upstairs. 'Has he been giving you a hard time?'

But this question was ignored as Elspeth asked one of her own. 'Is that really Duncan Sinclair downstairs? Was he waiting on the doorstep?'

'No, we met in the library. Apparently, it's been arranged that he will be helping with Leo Adare's biography. Ralph arranged this but forgot to tell me, so I've been behaving like a proper idiot.' And as she reached the top of the stairs, 'I'm sorry about Ralph.'

'Stop wasting your breath on apologies. He's not the same man. He doesn't realise what he's saying when he can speak.' To Isabel's surprise, Elspeth put her arm around her friend's waist and gazed at her intently. 'We both know the final outcome; however, it's you who needs some TLC. When did you last look in the mirror, go to the hairdresser, buy yourself a new dress?'

'And give Ralph more cause for complaint? Besides, I haven't time for such frivolities.'

'Stop talking like an old woman. You're up at the crack of dawn working on that biography. I'm glad a nurse now comes in to wash and shave Ralph. If he wasn't so bad-tempered, and I suppose that's to be expected, I'd suggest that she, or another nurse, come in for a few hours during the afternoon.'

'Giving him something else to grumble about.' Isabel sighed. 'Anyhow, I must go and see him. Duncan is coming up presently.'

'In that case, I'll make some tea, although he might prefer something stronger.'

It was some twenty minutes later that Duncan handed Elspeth his cup for replenishment. 'Thanks. Although we had some tea with Mr Elliott, I needed that.' And helping himself to another slice of fruit cake, 'This is delicious.'

Elspeth grinned. 'Good. Although I enjoy proofreading as my main occupation, cooking makes a pleasant change. You must come for a meal one evening,' but as her gaze turned to Isabel, who was crumbling her slice of cake, her expression changed.

'I'll look forward to it.' Duncan stood up, noting there was no comment from Isabel, whose attention was now focused on pushing currants and sultanas into little piles. 'It's good to see both of you again. I just wish it wasn't under such sad circumstances. Anyhow, I'll see you both in the morning.'

'Is Isabel unwell or just worried about Ralph?' enquired Duncan as he and Elspeth reached the front door.

'It's worry. We all know Ralph was very awkward even when he enjoyed good health, and that the

Alzheimer's is responsible for his bad temper and mood swings. The doctor said only yesterday that in Ralph's case the deterioration is unusually rapid.'

'He certainly didn't recognise me today and told me to get out. Then, after I spoke about Guernsey, that in spite of working on my novel I had enjoyed my stay there, he told me not to waste his or my time. To get on with more research on Leo.'

'That's exactly how he treats us, with the result that Isabel's only interested in work.'

'She certainly looked terrible at that party on Monday. And she doesn't look any better today.'

Elspeth still looked worried, but this didn't prevent her from asking, 'Was your trip a success? Did you finish your book? Meet Terence Yorke?'

'Yes to all three questions. I'll bring my notes on Terence tomorrow; but unless there's an improvement, I doubt that Ralph will understand. And I'll tell you more about Terence and Guernsey on another occasion.'

'I'm surprised that such a gregarious actor has settled in Guernsey.'

'He really loves it there. And I must say I enjoyed my stay on the island…'

Duncan had been surprised that he should meet

the retired actor so soon after he had completed his historical novel. He had learnt from the manager of the hotel in which he was staying that Terence was a regular lunchtime customer at a well-known hotel in St Peter Port, where he entertained the locals with amusing incidents from his theatrical career.

On entering the bar, Duncan had immediately recognised the voice – well-known to many Stratford-upon-Avon and West End theatre-goers – but was amazed at the transfiguration; a rust-coloured moustache and bushy beard concealed the well-shaped lips and determined jaw. A frown creased the famous brow while a pair of brilliant blue eyes met and held Duncan's before he could even order a drink. He had met Terence on various occasions and wondered if, despite his own collar-length hair and roughly-grown beard, Terence had recognised him. As the conversation continued, one of the business-suited locals turned to Duncan, 'Enjoying your holiday?'

'It's a lovely island, everyone is so friendly,' interrupted Terence. 'I'm really pleased I've bought a place of my own.'

'We certainly enjoy your company,' said the man who had spoken to Duncan and was still looking at him questioningly when Duncan murmured, 'Yes, it's very relaxing.'

'I know you,' said Terence a few minutes later, after the regulars had finished their drinks and returned to work. And as he seated himself next to Duncan, 'You're Sinclair, you write those marvellous historical novels. What are you doing in Guernsey? Working on something based locally?' And before Duncan could reply, 'You're a friend of Ralph McGuire, the biographer?'

'Yes. We've known each other a long time.'

'I hear he's suffering from Alzheimer's. Pity – he's a brilliant writer. I believe he's working on Adare's biography. Leo and I were contemporaries, often appeared in the same plays.'

Duncan knew that Terence had been devastated when, three years ago, his girlfriend (who had been appearing in the same play) had collapsed and died in his arms, on the stage. The other actors and audience had been deeply shocked and many theatre-goers were saddened to learn that Terence intended to leave the stage and England. He had wandered aimlessly around Europe, found himself in Guernsey where, due to the considerable fortune left to him by his grandmother, he bought a house.

Terence finished his drink and placed the glass on the counter. 'The last I heard was that due to Ralph's illness you'll be working on the biography with his wife, Isabel,' And again, before Duncan could confirm or deny this, Terence continued, 'I'm surprised I haven't been asked for any anecdotes or reminiscences.'

Duncan suppressed a sigh of relief, glad that Terence wouldn't be so surprised at his request. He had been told of the actor's friendship with the family who lived next door and that it was through them he had gradually regained his natural exuberance. The ten-year-old daughter, who was recovering from injuries sustained in a nasty car accident, had somehow found her way into his garden and into his heart. Two days later, with her parents' permission, Terence was encouraging her to speak.

'I was going to phone you; however, now I've met you, can we arrange a time that would be convenient?'

'Of course, I'd be delighted. Tomorrow afternoon at my place on the west coast.'

A time having been arranged and directions given, Duncan watched as Terence paused on the pavement outside the hotel, smiling and joking with various local people as they passed. It was obvious he was liked and respected by the islanders; nevertheless, Duncan wondered what Terence had meant when he said, 'Adare can be an awkward bugger at times, has strange companions. Have there been any adverse comments from any of Leo's colleagues?'

4

'This is all fantastic, just what we need.' Isabel looked up from Duncan's notes, unaware that he and Elspeth had been grinning at each other when she laughed at some of the anecdotes that Terence Yorke had recounted.

'I'm glad you like them. He's a great raconteur and will be only too pleased to furnish us with more, if needed.' Duncan had not enquired about Ralph but now asked, 'How's Ralph this morning?'

'Not very well, but hopefully he'll improve during the day,' said Isabel.

'What does the doctor say? Would stronger medication help?'

'I doubt it. Dr Beresford did tell us that in some cases the symptoms are worse than others.' Isabel looked across at Elspeth. 'I'm surprised the nurses tolerate his barbs and criticisms. He was really rude to the one that came yesterday.'

'I suppose she's accustomed to awkward patients.' Elspeth glanced at Duncan. 'Ralph usually has a rest after he's been washed and shaved; however, I'm sure he'll be pleased to see you.'

'Did you get any sleep at all last night?' asked Elspeth as the door closed and when Isabel shook her head, 'why don't you go and lie down on my bed for a couple of hours?' Elspeth's bedroom was at the end of the landing, furthest away from Ralph's room, and if the door was closed Isabel wouldn't hear if Ralph called out or rang his bell. 'Duncan and I are here if Ralph wants anything.'

'Thank you, but no. He's my husband. It's my duty to care for him.'

'Which is impossible when he disturbs you in the early hours.'

A few minutes later, Isabel crept upstairs and along the landing. She had been too tired to argue or protest and was glad to hear Ralph's mumbled comment and then Duncan talking about his stay in Guernsey. It only took a second to kick off her shoes, slide her skirt down over now-slender hips and creep under the duvet. The warmth, and the fragrance from the bowl of potpourri on the bedside table, were relaxing, and in an instant Isabel was asleep.

Meanwhile, Ralph was getting fractious and glared at Duncan. 'Why are you sitting there doing nothing?' Although his speech was slurred, he continued, 'There's more interviews to arrange, more of Leo's colleagues and friends who wish to contribute.' Ralph paused, no sound coming from his moving lips then, 'Some of it may be useless but that's for me to decide. In the meantime, you and Isabel can see these people.' It was as Duncan reached the door that Ralph's voice suddenly became stronger. 'Tell Isabel I want her, NOW!'

Elspeth was waiting at the foot of the stairs and on hearing of Ralph's request retorted indignantly, 'Isabel's asleep and I'm certainly not disturbing her.'

Then as she started up the stairs, 'I'll think of a suitable excuse by the time I reach his room.'

Alone in the study, Duncan scrutinised the list of actors and actresses whom Ralph wanted him or Isabel to interview, and the theatres in which they were currently appearing. While some were in London, others were scattered round the country: Birmingham, Stratford-upon-Avon and Chichester. Their addresses, the theatres and the respective telephone numbers were all neatly listed and Duncan considered that, subject to their availability, he would drive up to Birmingham, go on to Stratford and then down to London. Duncan dialled the Birmingham number and the actor, who had met Ralph on various occasions and knew of his illness, quickly said he would be delighted to contribute. At Stratford, directors and producers were also included, but only one was prepared to see Duncan while, after agreeing, two of the actors commented that they could also relate other stories which Adare would probably prefer to remain unknown.

'It's only Friday and you've already spoken to them all and made the necessary arrangements,' said Isabel, noting the dates and times written against each name.

'Yes, apart from three producers – two who weren't available and one who's on holiday – everyone was very co-operative. I'll leave early Monday morning, stay with my cousin in Birmingham overnight, and see the two actors in Stratford on Tuesday. It's a pity you can't do the London trip. It would do you good to—'

'Ralph needs me here,' interrupted Isabel. 'In any case, he asked you to go.'

Elspeth looked from one to the other and although relieved that Isabel looked better for an undisturbed sleep, was glad she had arranged a surprise for her friend. Pushing the cheeseboard towards Duncan so that he could help himself, she told Isabel, 'Joanna's coming to see Ralph tomorrow afternoon and I've arranged a hair appointment for you – my treat.'

'There's no need…' began Isabel, pushing her straggly hair behind her ears then, aware of Duncan's gaze, 'I'm sorry, I didn't mean to sound ungrateful. It's very kind and thoughtful of you. I must admit I haven't bothered about my appearance recently.'

You've worn the same skirt for the last three weeks, thought Elspeth. *And would have worn the first dress at hand for the party if I hadn't looked out a black cocktail dress*. Even so, this had hung on Isabel and looking at her, anyone would think it was she who was ill, not Ralph. There was nothing wrong with his eyesight; he must have noticed her drastic weight loss.

'A stairlift would certainly make life easier for both of you,' said Duncan. 'Ralph could then spend part of the day downstairs, thus saving you time and energy.' Then, as it occurred to him, 'How on earth did you manage Monday evening?'

'With the help of a male nurse and with great difficulty,' said Elspeth while Isabel added, 'Ralph was very adamant in his refusal when we suggested a stairlift. Joanna, who's his niece, tried to persuade him but he was really rude to her.'

'That's a pity.' Duncan pushed back his chair and stood up. 'Thanks for lunch, it was most enjoyable,' and glancing at Isabel who was pushing a small piece of cheese around her plate, 'has anything been decided about photographs to be used in Adare's biography?'

'Leo has chosen several, all in costume when playing supporting roles, but Hugo isn't very happy with his choice. They're meeting next week to discuss them.'

'What about some when he was a child, his role in the school play when his potential was recognised?'

'It's possible his aunts who live in Sidmouth may have some.' Isabel picked up Duncan's and her own plate. 'Ralph wants me to read him the first six chapters to make sure nothing has been omitted.'

'That's highly unlikely,' said Elspeth. 'Besides, you read them to him only ten days ago.'

Isabel shrugged. 'He can't remember that, and if it makes him happy, I don't mind.'

'You're marvellous, and I'm sorry he doesn't appreciate everything you're doing for him.' Then, as the thought occurred to her, 'He'll probably fall asleep and then want you to start that particular chapter again.'

'I don't mind.'

What's Ralph going to say? thought Isabel as she gazed at her reflection and then up at the stylist who said, 'It looks lovely and the style suits you.'

Isabel's dark brown hair had been shoulder-length but now, considerably shorter, fell in soft curls about her ears. The girl knew of Ralph's illness and thoughtfully refrained from saying that he probably wouldn't even notice. Instead, she said, 'Come and see us again soon, just for a trim. I'm sure you'll find it much easier to look after now it's short.'

'Isabel, you've had your hair cut! It looks lovely,' exclaimed Joanna, who was standing in the hall while

Elspeth nodded approvingly, at the same time thinking that if she couldn't persuade Isabel to buy some new clothes she would have to do something about it herself. She then heard Isabel thank Joanna for visiting Ralph.

'That's no problem. At first, he was quite talkative then he became rather confused, thought I was you, then Elspeth. I told him that I'll come again next week but I doubt that he'll remember, so if you want to do anything in connection with the current biography or just go out for a drive, please do. A complete change would do you good.'

'Thanks, but I expect it'll be a visit to the library.'

5

Isabel placed the printed chapters in a manila folder, pushed this aside and reached for the notes which Duncan had assiduously researched.

They had both been surprised to learn that Leo Adare had indulged in relationships with younger men and expressed curiosity about his current partner. Isabel had spoken to Hugo Forrester about this, but he was unable to offer any information about Leo's private life. He had, however, suggested that Duncan might learn something from one of Leo's contemporaries when he met them.

Isabel nodded approvingly as she read Duncan's notes again. As usual, they were concise and brief and she was glad that, even though it was Sunday morning, she had done this. She had intended to do this the previous day, but Ralph had become fractious during the morning, demanding her time and attention, frustrated that he was unable to communicate.

And now he's dead, thought Isabel, worried that the bottle containing Ralph's tablets was empty. What had happened to them? There was no way Ralph could get to the bathroom and Joanna had assured the chief inspector that the only time she had left her uncle had been to answer the doorbell. It was obvious they would all be questioned again. In the meantime, the post-mortem would be the next day, Monday, and the inquest later in the week.

Leo Adare finished reading the review, grunted, and threw the paper in the corner. He had been surprised to learn that Zak Amory, his young protégé and later lover, had a supporting role at the Old Vic in Bristol and was receiving glowing reviews.

For a moment, Zak's face flashed before him, his jet-black hair cut short and spiky, the bright green eyes and the cheeky grin, and Leo briefly considered a visit to the Old Vic while on his next visit to his cottage in the Mendips. Shifting in his armchair, Leo grunted again, knowing that such a visit would incite his current lover's wrath and Dominic, for all his loving ways, could be vicious. He had never known his predecessor's name and profession, and it was wiser for things to stay that way.

Easing his large, overweight frame into a more comfortable position, Leo turned his thoughts to his biography and Ralph McGuire. He had known from his weekly phone call to Isabel – sometimes he spoke to Elspeth – that Ralph's condition was deteriorating and had been sorry to learn of his death the previous afternoon, and surprised to hear of the police presence.

He had been advised by Isabel that Duncan Sinclair would be doing the necessary research while she would be doing the actual writing and agreed to this plan of action. He had also approved the actors, directors and producers to be interviewed and knew that Isabel would reject any adverse comments.

Leo sighed. He knew his main problem had been and still was his behaviour with some of the young men with whom he had formed relationships. This had caused considerable comment, but Leo reflected that the antics of some of the older actors with young starlets and nymphets were almost grotesque. He was also aware that there were those who were jealous of his success and would resent the publicity caused by his biography but was sure that, despite Ralph's death, Isabel would complete this to his satisfaction.

Meanwhile, in his tiny flat in Bristol, Zak Amory was reading the same review, his sensuous lips curving into a mischievous grin. He had been dejected and furious when Leo told him to get out. Their affair was ended, but despite this, he promised himself a successful future on TV or the stage. Unbeknown to Leo, he had auditioned for a role in a popular and well-known soap and, within ten days of leaving Leo, he had received a call asking him to report to the studio the following Monday.

That had been two years ago; however, on learning that this character was being written out, Zak had kept his eyes and ears open. He had heard two of the older actors talking about the production of a controversial thriller in Bristol and that the casting director was looking around for a young male actor. At the audition, his portrayal of characters from Shakespeare, Ibsen, Ayckbourn and Tom Stoppard earnt him unexpected praise; he was given the script of the new play and told to spend the next three days studying this. On his return, and after an exhausting morning playing the part of a scheming, malevolent fraudster, he was questioned about his friendship with Leo Adare. This had come as a shock, as only the day before he had read an article about Leo and seen a photograph of him with his black lover, which still infuriated him.

Three days later, when he had almost given up hope, he was offered the role, told that rehearsals would begin in a fortnight and to find himself accommodation in Bristol. Zak was surprised to learn that it was his facial expressions and body language, when questioned about Adare, which actually won him the role.

Cutting out the review so that it could be pasted in his scrapbook, Zak reflected it was strange that, on the second day of rehearsals, he should meet Kieran O'Brien, Leo's nephew. Still elated that he had been chosen for this particular role, Zak had decided to celebrate by having dinner at one of the large hotels near the centre. The fact that he would be dining alone did not deter him.

On arrival at the restaurant, Kieran had greeted him with a friendly smile and later enquired if he lived in Bristol or was passing through, then, on learning of Zak's success, had offered his congratulations. Later that evening, after Kieran had finished work and they met at a nearby pub, Zak learnt that Leo Adare was Kieran's uncle. The play had now been running three months and during that time they had become good friends.

It was midday when Detective Inspector Kershaw learnt that Duncan Sinclair would be returning early that evening. Elspeth also told him that Joanna would be staying with them for a few days and would be available for further questioning late that afternoon. Keen to meet Sinclair and not wanting to waste time, Kershaw said that if Duncan had not arrived when he called, he would speak to Joanna first. He also intended to visit Alex Gresham (who lived opposite the McGuires and had been very helpful on Saturday) again, but in the meantime there was a post-mortem to attend.

Once again, Kershaw was astounded at his young sergeant's stamina as they watched the gory procedure and, for a moment, his thoughts strayed. He had noticed Tom's enthusiasm when, as a constable, his observation had helped in arresting the team responsible for stealing valuable articles which had been included in some of the *Antique Road Show* programmes.

As usual, the pathologist described everything in detail stating that, while his report would be on the inspector's desk the next morning, Tuesday, it would be some time before he received the results of the further tests which would be carried out.

'Who do you think did it?' asked Tom as he drove back to the station and, when there was no immediate reply, 'could Isabel have done it before she went out?'

'It's possible, although I doubt it. We don't know, of course, how long it would take Ralph to lose consciousness after an overdose had been administered, whether it would be immediate. Joanna said that Ralph was fully conscious when she went up to see him – that was as soon as she arrived and after Isabel had gone out.'

'What about Elspeth, or even Joanna?' asked Tom.

'Doubtful. According to Elspeth, she went straight out when Joanna suggested it. She had no reason to go upstairs and, as for Joanna, she was very upset.'

'H'm,' grunted Tom. 'I thought she was overdoing it.'

'Time will tell. It's a pity that Alex Gresham is the only neighbour who saw this mysterious caller. Hopefully, he may have remembered something else by the time we see him later today.'

'Perhaps Hugo Forrester will be able to help us,' suggested Tom.

'I'm not pinning much faith on his visit.'

'I'm sorry I can't tell you anything about Ralph's private life, friends or even acquaintances,' said Hugo after he had expressed his shock over Ralph's sudden death. He had come straight from seeing Isabel and Elspeth and now resumed, 'I knew Ralph was ill, but I was really shaken when Isabel phoned me on Saturday. However, I would like to know what happened.'

'So would we. The post-mortem was earlier this afternoon, but we have to wait for the result of further tests.'

'Why is Ralph's bedroom sealed?'

'Although our team spent the remainder of Saturday and part of yesterday there, it may be necessary for them to return. However, you've known Ralph a long time, is there anything we should know?'

'I didn't see him very often and while Isabel has never complained, I had the impression that he could be a difficult man. I must admit I was surprised when he married. I don't think there was any affection on his side, but Ralph obviously knew that Isabel was very intelligent and a hard worker. This soon became clear when, in addition to doing all the research, Isabel was writing most of the biographies. I realise that one should never speak ill of the dead, but not once did he include her in the acknowledgements, or offer any praise at any of the launch parties. However, I'll make sure that she now receives the acclaim due to her. I'm really pleased that Duncan Sinclair is going to help her.'

'Sinclair,' echoed Kershaw. 'I'm seeing him this evening, but in the meantime, what can you tell me about him?'

'How can I help you, Inspector?' Alex Gresham, who lived in the ground floor flat of the house opposite the McGuires, ushered the two detectives into his sparsely furnished living room and waited until they were seated.

'Would you mind repeating the description of the person who called at the McGuire house on Saturday?' Kershaw occupied the armchair which faced the window and therefore the road, assuming this was where Gresham usually sat.

'It was the clothes that attracted my attention.' Gresham sat in an identical chair facing the Inspector, adjusted his glasses and resumed. 'The wide-brimmed hat was pulled down as far as it would go, the scarf concealed the lower part of the face while the coat made it impossible to tell if he was fat or thin. But he must be fit.' Gresham then said that the caller had approached from the right. He was walking quite fast and obviously knew where he was going. He didn't pause or hesitate until he reached the house when he rang the bell. 'I couldn't see who opened the door, but he almost knocked them over as he entered.'

'Did you see him leave?'

'No, Inspector. I admit I was curious but I'm not a curtain-twitcher. It just happened that I was working on an article for the *National Geographic Magazine*, which had to be sent off that evening, and my notes were on that table.' Gresham indicated notebooks and several sheets of typescript.

'That's a pity. It would have been useful if you had seen him full face. Unfortunately, Joanna McGuire can't tell us any more than you. However, have you ever seen this man before?'

'Not to my knowledge, but he probably looks very different when wearing a business suit or casual clothes. He must have been hot wearing that heavy coat.'

Tom, who had been sat on the upright chair near the window, looked across at Kershaw waiting for further questions but none were forthcoming. Instead, the inspector nodded in his direction and stood up. 'Thank you for your assistance, Mr Gresham. Should you think of anything else or see this man again, I'd be glad if you could let me know.'

'Of course, but tell me, Inspector; how is Mrs McGuire?'

'She's very upset naturally, but Elspeth is most supportive.'

'Ah, Elspeth.' Alex Gresham smiled knowingly. 'A clever and very attractive woman. I'm surprised she stayed on when Ralph married.'

'What do you mean?'

'Ralph had a terrible temper and even in those days, on a fine day when the windows were open, you could hear him shouting at her. My wife was alive at the time, knew that Elspeth worked from home and would often ask her over for a cup of tea or coffee. They had a succession of housekeepers until Ralph married when Elspeth, who is an excellent cook and enjoys it, suggested she cook the evening meal and arrange domestic help on a daily basis. However, I'm sure you don't want to hear all this trivia?'

'It's most interesting. Do you know how long Ralph has lived there?'

'Always. He and Elspeth lived there as children, so presumably it was left to them by their parents.'

Kershaw nodded, expressed his thanks again and as they crossed the road to the McGuire household hazarded, 'I wonder who stands to benefit from Ralph's death.'

6

'I don't understand it. Ralph couldn't possibly have got to the bathroom, and why should this unexpected visitor, who should never have been allowed upstairs, want to…?' Isabel's voice faded.

'That's a question we're asking ourselves, Mrs McGuire.' Detective Inspector Kershaw noted her pale face and spoke quietly. 'I realise this is very upsetting for you and that I've asked you before: do you remember anyone who wears a fedora, a dark green scarf and Austrian-style overcoat?'

'No. As you already know, Ralph had few visitors even when he was well; he was always absorbed in his work. Since the Alzheimer's began, he didn't want to see anyone, and I can only assume that this person had a cold or didn't want to be recognised.' Once again Isabel's gaze travelled to the sergeant and then back to the inspector. 'What did he hope to gain?'

'That's what we would like to know.' There had been no indication that the contents of the chest of drawers or wardrobe had been disturbed, but this did not prevent Kershaw from saying, 'Should you discover that anything is missing, please let me know at once. And now, if it's convenient, I'd like to speak to Joanna.'

Subdued and still upset, Joanna repeated what she had said on Saturday and then suddenly asked, 'Have you found the hat and scarf? Or the man?'

'No, but we're still looking and questioning neighbours. So far we've only spoken to one. It's unfortunate that most of the people living nearby were out.'

Joanna nodded. 'It was a lovely afternoon which probably accounts for that. As you've no doubt seen for yourself, most of the houses have been converted into flats. This is one of the few houses still occupied by a family.'

In reply to Kershaw's further questions, Joanna told him that Ralph had never entertained or been entertained by any of the neighbours.

'I doubt that he knew their names. When writing, he almost became a recluse.' Joanna briefly said that Ralph had written two series for television about aristocratic families and their homes, and then went on to biographies. 'Isabel has been absolutely marvellous. Even before he was ill she was running here and there for him. Although he was my uncle and I shouldn't say it, he was a miserable and ungrateful bugger. Never a word of praise or a "thank you". I was always glad that Elspeth continued to live here; she stood up to Ralph.'

Kershaw knew that Joanna was head receptionist at a well-known hotel, hence her concise statement,

43

and now said, 'Thank you, Joanna. That was most interesting and has given us an insight into the McGuire household. One further question, did your uncle have any enemies? Was there anyone who disliked him so intensely that they would—?'

'No,' interrupted Joanna and then relented. 'I suppose it's possible. If I can think of anyone I'll certainly let you know.'

A few minutes later, Detective Inspector Kershaw greeted Duncan Sinclair with his usual courteous manner, at the same time aware that Detective Sergeant Small had quickly adjusted his expression of astonishment. Kershaw had also expected an older man and guessed the tall, handsome man to be in his mid-forties. And without wasting time he said, 'I realise you've only recently returned to England and were away from Bristol on Saturday. However, do you know anyone, i.e. Ralph's visitor, who would wear a hat, scarf and heavy overcoat at this time of year?'

'No. In fact, I doubt that I can be of any assistance to you at all, Inspector.' Kershaw then learnt of Duncan's surprise when Ralph asked him to help with the necessary research on his return to England. 'I was even more surprised, when I met Isabel in the library, to hear that she knew nothing about this arrangement. I was angry that Ralph didn't have the courtesy to tell her.'

'But despite this, you were and remained on good terms with Ralph for the short time between your return and departure for Birmingham?'

'It was only a few days, but yes. Ralph was keen that I should interview more of Leo's contemporaries.' Duncan then learnt that the empty bottle in the bathroom cabinet was being tested for fingerprints and that the scene of crime team had nearly finished.

'It's been a long...'

Kershaw broke off as a uniformed constable knocked and entered. 'Excuse me, sir, one of the officers from the house-to-house team would like a word.' Realising the inspector was unlikely to impart any further information, Duncan headed for the kitchen.

Meanwhile, upstairs, the officer in charge was checking that nothing had been overlooked. In addition to the bedroom and its contents, the bathroom cabinet, wash basin and every other surface had also been dusted for fingerprints. Small plastic envelopes contained various miniscule fibres, and it was hoped that these did not pertain to the bed coverings, chairs, curtains or carpets. It had been ascertained that the room had been kept at an even temperature; so hopefully, the visitor had removed his hat, scarf and coat in which case some evidence of these might be found.

'We're not doing very well, are we, sir?' said Tom.

'No, but we've done enough for today. I'll just tell Mrs McGuire we're going.' During a further conversation, Joanna had told them she was unable to add anything to her previous description. It had been impossible for her to see if the caller had a moustache, beard or had been clean-shaven; neither could she tell them the colour of his hair. He had been taller than her – Joanna guessed about 5' 10" – but because of the coat, she couldn't say if he was fat or thin.

However, before Kershaw could reach the kitchen Isabel emerged. 'Would you like a coffee before you go, Inspector?'

'No, thank you.' Kershaw had previously mentioned that he had an appointment to see Peter Hoskins, Ralph's solicitor, the following morning and now asked, 'Will you be attending the inquest on Wednesday?'

'Yes. Joanna will be working but Duncan is coming with us.'

Peter Hoskins greeted Detective Inspector Kershaw and Detective Sergeant Small with a courteous smile. 'I'm not very happy about giving you the information you require, Inspector. However, you did emphasise that it could help with your enquiries.'

'It could provide a motive, especially if any of the suspects are in financial difficulties.'

'You don't surely think that Mrs McGuire was responsible for her husband's death?'

'We're checking everyone's alibi.' Isabel had spent an hour at the library where she had been seen by the head librarian and some of the staff. The time of her arrival and departure had been rechecked and, while Kershaw knew that Ralph had become a tyrant, he doubted that Isabel would think up the ploy which had caused his death. Besides, there was nothing of that particular shade of green in her wardrobe which matched the miniscule fibres.

Kershaw leant back in his chair as Hoskins began. 'Isabel is the main beneficiary while Elspeth and Joanna receive substantial bequests.' Then, in reply to Kershaw's query, 'There are no other relatives and Ralph wasn't in favour of leaving money to deserving charities.'

Hoskins' gaze travelled to Tom and back to Kershaw. 'Isabel inherits the house, Ralph's portfolio of stocks and shares, and the residue of the estate which makes her a wealthy widow.'

'What did you think of Hoskins' last remark?' asked Tom as they regained the pavement.

'Strange, almost as though he disapproves of Isabel's good fortune. It's possible Elspeth will be disappointed about the house, but it was left up to Ralph, who has probably left her a reasonable legacy.' Kershaw indicated a nearby brasserie. 'Let's have a coffee break,' and once they were seated and their order given, he continued, 'if it wasn't for Gresham's statement you could almost think the caller was a figment of Joanna's imagination. We know she has a good job and is extremely efficient, but we don't know what her financial situation is. That's another thing to be checked, also Elspeth's.'

'What about the green fibres?' queried Tom.

'He, assuming it's a man, must have taken his coat off, even for a few minutes – it was really warm in that bedroom. Or perhaps he wanted to wash his hands.' A smiling buxom waitress set down their cappuccinos when the two men smiled their thanks and Kershaw resumed, 'I'll continue checking the contents of Ralph's desk while you carry on reading what has already been written about Adare, and Isabel's notes.'

Kershaw sipped his coffee appreciatively while Tom asked, 'Do you really think this is relevant?'

'I can't help wondering if Ralph's death is somehow connected with Adare's biography. You must admit this caller sounds rather theatrical. He arrives overdressed, almost forces his way in and, without asking, goes up to Ralph's—'

'Could it have been a woman?' interrupted Tom. 'It's not as though any physical strength was necessary, and it's often women who resort to poison or overdoses. But why?'

Kershaw shrugged. 'We only know of three women and I doubt that Joanna would have recognised Isabel or Elspeth dressed like that. The clothes could have been hired from a fancy dress shop.' Kershaw stopped abruptly. 'No, I don't think that's really possible. Isabel was seated at the same table all the time she was in the library while Elspeth was wearing a smart suit that afternoon. She wasn't out all that long, didn't use the car. However, it would be a useful exercise to check on fancy dress suppliers.'

Half an hour later, Tom replaced the receiver and muttered, 'No luck but I have had another idea. Perhaps it's someone connected with the theatre, maybe a person who's jealous or dislikes Adare and doesn't want this biography to be written. He could have borrowed the items from the theatre wardrobe. Shall I make enquiries?'

'No, get someone else to do it. Duncan Sinclair is due and may need to explain what he's giving you to read.'

'Don't worry,' it's not as bad as it looks.' Duncan placed two bulky files in front of Tom and continued, 'The first file contains a copy of the script,' and glancing at the inspector, 'Isabel would like to know when we can move back into the study.'

Kershaw had examined the contents of Ralph's desk, studied the titles of reference books on the shelves, and photographs of the various people about whom Ralph had written, but in spite of this he said, 'I'll come round this afternoon but you can move back tomorrow.'

'Thank you. However, I doubt that Isabel will feel inclined to work; it's the inquest in the morning,' and when there was no immediate response, 'Elspeth and Isabel were asking about the funeral.'

'If the coroner agrees that the body can be released they can make the necessary arrangements.'

As anticipated, the inquest was adjourned and the coroner agreed that Ralph's body could be released for burial. During the proceedings it was established that Ralph could not have reached the bathroom and that the overdose had been administered by person/s unknown.

Kershaw had noted that Isabel had remained calm and Elspeth tense, and watched as they emerged from the coroner's court followed by Dr Beresford. Duncan Sinclair, who had left earlier, drew up at the kerb as Kershaw approached Isabel and said quietly, 'You'll be able to go ahead with the funeral arrangements now, Mrs McGuire.'

'Yes, but…' Isabel looked uncertain. 'We still don't know what happened. Who the caller was.'

'That's what we have to find out.' As he drove back to the station, Kershaw wondered if Tom had found anything which would help them with their enquiries. Was the caller a man or a woman?

Kershaw's thoughts then turned to his conversation with Dr Beresford. The doctor had told him that Ralph McGuire had not been prescribed the latest drug for Alzheimer's but had been taking an old-fashioned anti-depressant. An overdose of this would cause strange heartbeats, and death. Had the caller known this, or anticipated that an overdose of whatever medication had been prescribed for Ralph would hasten his death?

7

'Pleasant service, sir. I didn't expect to see so many people there.'

Detective Inspector Kershaw was surprised as Detective Sergeant Rowena Lovell, one of the team who had carried out the house-to-house enquiries, joined him to watch the cars drive away from the church. 'Judging from appearances I would say some were contemporaries from McGuire's college days, while others were certainly from the theatre.'

Rowena nodded. 'Was Mr Adare there or any other actors whose biographies Mr McGuire wrote?'

'I don't know but the funeral director is sending me a list of those who attended.'

'You might recognise some of them if you go back to the house,' suggested Rowena and quickly added, 'I'm pleased to see that Mrs McGuire is looking better. It's not easy caring for someone with Alzheimer's – I've an uncle who has it. My cousin, who's taking compassionate leave until she can make alternative arrangements, finds it very difficult. I relieve her whenever I can, but he doesn't always recognise me. There's such a personality change, and at times he's very confused.'

Kershaw glanced at the slim young woman standing beside him, reflecting that he knew very little about the private life of those in his team and said, 'So you could understand Isabel's concern?'

'Yes, but she tolerated Ralph's demanding and selfish ways long before he was ill. His behaviour in the library, on the occasions he went himself, was general knowledge.'

'That's very interesting,' but as he walked towards the car park, Kershaw considered that he must read Rowena's notes again. Although Isabel said it was unnecessary, Rowena had spent the Saturday evening and all day Sunday at the house, thereby acquiring useful information.

It was Elspeth who opened the door and greeted Kershaw. 'Come in, Inspector. Isabel will be pleased you're here – perhaps you'll meet someone who can help you with your enquiries.'

Kershaw looked past Elspeth into the crowded lounge, quickly noting that a table had been placed in the centre of the room while the two large settees and various armchairs, all rather shabby, had been pushed against the walls, but many people were standing. For a moment he watched as guests helped themselves to the food then transferred his gaze to the three women standing near the window. He immediately recognised the main spokeswoman, an elderly actress who, despite her age, still looked elegant and distinguished. Accepting a glass of white wine from Joanna, who greeted him with a nervous smile, he made his way towards them, confident they would be happy to talk about their careers and Ralph.

Within minutes, Kershaw found himself being entertained, each describing Ralph's irrelevant and sometimes sensitive questions, all concluding that they were delighted with their biographies. At last, he was able to ask, 'Is Leo Adare here?'

'No, thank goodness,' snapped the second actress, who was short, stout and had untidy hair.

'His fans probably think he's marvellous but he's not a very nice man,' offered the third actress with varicoloured frizzy hair. 'Backstage, he's ill-mannered and rude. It's surprising he still has the same dresser.'

'He could probably tell a few tales, especially about Dominic, his latest lover.' This came from the first actress and glancing at Kershaw she elaborated, 'He's black and has acquired a niche for himself as a portrait painter.'

'I'm sure Ralph or Isabel has spoken to Leo's dresser,' said the second.

'But there's one person who wouldn't want to be asked for a contribution.' The elegant actress looked across at Kershaw as though she knew him personally, and his profession. 'His nephew.'

'Kieran O'Brien, who happens to live in Bristol and is restaurant manager at a well-known hotel. He certainly doesn't like his uncle.' The second actress grinned maliciously, revealing yellowing teeth. 'Apparently, he's told Leo that a biography is unnecessary and asked if the truth about his uncle's private life and behaviour was going to be included.'

'Aren't you forgetting where you are, Miranda?' scolded the first actress. 'You shouldn't talk like that. I'm sure this gentleman isn't interested,' and glancing at Kershaw she enquired, 'are you a relative or friend?'

Aware that the other two women were also gazing at him with curiosity, Kershaw told them, 'An acquaintance; and I must speak to Isabel before I leave.'

But before he could reach her, Elspeth greeted him with, 'Did you enjoy your conversation with the old dears who play the three witches in *Macbeth*?'

'It was very enlightening.' Kershaw noticed that Isabel, wearing a smart black suit, was talking to two scholarly-looking men and nodded when Elspeth told him they were colleagues from Ralph's years at the college of further education. She added that Isabel would probably appreciate his intervention.

Although very pale, Isabel greeted him with a smile. 'It was very kind of you to attend the funeral,' then, interrupting the flow of conversation, 'Mr Kershaw is a family friend.'

'In that case, we'll leave you together,' said the two men simultaneously and as they turned away, the bald-headed man said, 'If you need any advice or assistance when dealing with Ralph's affairs, please let us know.'

Isabel nodded and then looked up at Kershaw, 'Thank you for rescuing me.' And without pausing, 'Is there anyone here who can help you with your enquiries?'

Kershaw scanned the crowded room and learning that Ralph had not seen either of his university colleagues for the last five years, considered that this was not an opportune moment to ask about Leo's nephew or dresser and after commenting about the service and attendance, departed.

'Was it that boring?' Inspector Kershaw had opened his office door quietly, just as Detective Sergeant Small yawned and stretched.

'No. Most of it was quite interesting. However, were there many at the funeral? Did you go back to the house?'

Tom grinned as Kershaw told him about his

encounter with the three actresses and Ralph's college of further education colleagues, but his expression changed as Kershaw asked, 'What do you make of the notes about Adare's dresser?'

On learning that there weren't any on him or Kieran O'Brien, the inspector shook his head. 'Strange. I would have thought they were amongst the first to be interviewed.'

'They're not even on the list of those Duncan has yet to see,' said Tom.

'I wonder why. I'll ask Isabel about them tomorrow.'

A few minutes later, and looking very thoughtful, Kershaw asked himself, 'Who was that caller and, if he was responsible for Ralph's death, why?'

'Perhaps he's someone who anticipated a substantial legacy,' ventured Tom and when Kershaw shook his head, suggested, 'jealousy, revenge.'

'Why? Ralph led a very private life since he became a biographer.' Kershaw studied the statements given by the three women who had been in the house on that Saturday afternoon, noting yet again Joanna's arrival, Isabel's, then Elspeth's departure and Ralph's annoyance at the persistent ringing of the doorbell. He recalled Joanna's astonishment when asked about the bedroom furniture, in particular the chairs on either side of the bed and the bedside table; she thought these were in the same place as when she arrived. She had looked even more puzzled when questioned about the door leading to the bathroom and agreed this could have been pushed open – her main concern had been her uncle.

Isabel had confirmed that these items of furniture were in their usual place and that the bathroom door had been slightly ajar when she left. Dr Beresford's fingerprints were amongst those on the door and bathroom cabinet, while the bottle containing Ralph's medication had been wiped clean.

It was unfortunate that none of the wardrobe mistresses at the various theatres had been able to help, and the problem of identifying the hat, scarf and coat was still being pursued. Kershaw grunted with frustration when Tom looked up and offered, 'The clothes definitely sound Austrian. Perhaps the caller comes from there or bought those items while on holiday.'

'That's a good idea. I'll ask Isabel and Elspeth tomorrow.' Tom's suggestion that he should organise tea and biscuits was accepted with alacrity, and as the door closed behind him Kershaw leant back and considered that the McGuire household had been a strange one.

He had learnt from Isabel and Elspeth that Ralph had attended one of the lesser colleges of Oxford University where he acquired a degree in History, and followed this at a redbrick in Kent where he acquired an MA in Modern History. Ralph had then spent the following five years as a lecturer at a college of further education in Bournemouth and then moved back to Bristol where he held a similar position at another college of further education.

At the age of forty-one, he had negotiated a contract with the specialist publishers of which Hugo Forrester was the managing director, to write a series of six biographies of lesser-known actors. Isabel, highly intelligent and an academic in her own right, had taught English at her old school but somehow found time to assist Ralph with the research on the television series on aristocratic families.

Ralph was already beginning to suffer from Alzheimer's when they started on the third biography of the second contract so that Isabel had not only researched for this and the previous two biographies, but had written them. For a while, Ralph seemed to improve, and it was during this period that he met and agreed to write, certainly supervise, Leo Adare's biography. However, Ralph's rapidly accentuating dementia had thrown more responsibility onto Isabel's shoulders; she was working completely on her own and had been grateful for Elspeth's help and continued friendship. Kershaw considered that Isabel and Elspeth had both been very loyal when talking about Ralph. In spite of all the work she had done, Isabel had not complained or criticised, while Elspeth had merely said that Ralph was not an easy person to live with.

Kershaw silently admitted he had never heard of

Ralph McGuire until his death (he was not a reader of biographies) and that he had been surprised to learn that Duncan Sinclair, well-known author of historical novels and a younger man, was helping with the biography on Leo Adare. He had also been amazed that Isabel had not known of Ralph's arrangement with Sinclair – that this had been done while Duncan was in Guernsey. Once again, Kershaw considered it strange that this island should have a distant connection with one of his cases.

Duncan had said that although working on his book, he had thoroughly enjoyed his stay and hoped to return to Guernsey for a holiday at a later date.

Kershaw recalled Isabel saying that Ralph had become more confused and forgetful, disliked being dependent on them and the nurses, hated the commode being in the bedroom and dreaded becoming incontinent. She had also feared the inevitable – Ralph being hospitalised, the indignities he would have to suffer and stated adamantly that, despite this, she had not given him the overdose. Kershaw remembered that Elspeth had almost used the same words, and Joanna's suggestion that by admitting this stranger she was partially responsible for her uncle's death. Joanna had, of course, returned to her own flat, and now there was just Isabel and Elspeth living in that large house with all that old-fashioned furniture.

Kershaw's thoughts turned to the small terraced house in which he had been brought up. His parents had been strict but very affectionate; however, there was one thing for which he had never forgiven them: his name. To be christened Oswald was bad enough but with a surname like his, he was constantly ridiculed or called 'OK' by his classmates. It was after the death of his parents, who died in a car accident on a busy motorway, and at the age of nineteen that he decided to change his name but strangely enough chose 'Oliver'. He had thought about this for some time but did not want to hurt their feelings while they were alive. However, after obtaining the necessary letter from the family solicitor, he applied for a passport in the name of Oliver Kershaw. Since joining the force, he had been called by his surname, and those with whom he became friendly called him Oliver.

Over the years he had met and known a number of attractive girls and women but eventually discovered that none of them were prepared to tolerate the irregularity of his hours. There had been one particular young woman whom he had met through different investigations, but unfortunately, she was engaged and later married. He had immediately been attracted to Elspeth McGuire, amazed that such an attractive and intelligent woman should still be single and had decided that as soon as a satisfactory conclusion had been reached he would ask her out for a drink, or even dinner. In the meantime, he had to ascertain the identity of the mysterious visitor and if this person was responsible for Ralph's death.

8

'Who is this Kieran O'Brien and why is he asking me to dinner?'

Duncan noticed that Isabel was studying an identical invitation and raised his eyebrows as she told him, 'He's Leo Adare's nephew. But I can't go; it's too soon.'

'There's no reason why you shouldn't go. You've hardly been out of the house since the funeral. It would do you good to meet other people.'

'That's just it. I don't feel up to meeting other people, talking about Ralph, his death.'

Duncan nodded sympathetically. 'I'm sure Kieran will understand if you do decline.'

'I don't know that he will. On each occasion Ralph or I suggested that Kieran might like to contribute an interesting or amusing anecdote, even something about the family, Leo rejected the idea. He said that Kieran could be awkward.' Isabel studied the invitation again. 'It says small – that could be six or eight.'

'Ring and ask. Say you haven't been out since

Ralph's death so you're feeling rather apprehensive. Would you like me to phone?'

'No, I'll do it.'

Five minutes later, Isabel replaced the receiver. 'I didn't expect that; he sounded polite and quite charming. He suggests I wait until the day and if I don't feel up to it that morning, to let him know.'

'That's fair enough, but I can't back out. However, it will be interesting to meet him. Is he Leo's only relative?'

'No, there are two elderly aunts who live in Sidmouth. They're very sweet and most helpful; however, in spite of Leo's remarks, I must admit I'm rather curious about Kieran.'

At the same time that Isabel and Duncan were discussing Kieran's invitation, Marina Bushell, Kieran's partner, was muttering to herself, 'I can't understand Kieran having a party in a place like this.' Kieran had left early for the hotel and Marina now critically scrutinised the lounge and small dining area, still grumbling. 'It's not as though we've anything to show off – none of these people are friends. We know Belinda and Stefan because they're neighbours – their house is larger than this and everything about it is very luxurious, but why did he have to ask Isabel McGuire and Duncan Sinclair?'

Marina adjusted the curtains and peered out into the road. 'Although Ralph's dead, they're still working on this stupid biography of Leo Adare, but what am I going to get out of this party? Ralph must have been very rich living in a large house, double garage, so two cars, and she… Isabel probably has a wardrobe full of designer clothes.'

Marina had met Kieran six years ago, and a year later they had moved into the house at Henleaze. It was three months after they met that Marina learnt of Kieran's dislike for his uncle, Leo Adare, and that he did not approve of the biography which was being written by Ralph McGuire, but she had said nothing.

She had been eleven when she learnt that Ralph was her father and was hurt that he had never written to her, wanted to meet her. Her maternal grandparents, who had been affectionate, kind and never referred to him, were both dead by then and she had often wondered if they had known his name. Her mother and grandparents had been delighted at her flair for languages – she had received a good education, made a lot of friends who were envious of her fluency in French and German and often invited her to spend holidays abroad with them. Although she accepted and enjoyed these, she always considered that family holidays were an unknown luxury. Her mother had died a few days before her twentieth birthday.

Marina's thoughts reverted to Ralph and she muttered, 'Why should Isabel inherit everything?'

Marina had her birth certificate on which Ralph McGuire was named as her father, and letters that he had written to her mother, so there shouldn't be any difficulty in claiming against his estate.

Marina knew it was highly improbable that Leo – who at fifty-four was likely to die – in spite of owning a flat in London and cottage in the Mendips, would leave much to Kieran. Although she agreed that Kieran had good reason to dislike his uncle, he was the only blood relative, and it seemed a great pity that Leo should leave everything to whoever was his partner at the time. While she earned a reasonable wage and Kieran was as generous as his salary and the mortgage would allow, Marina thought how wonderful it must be to live in a large house (she had walked past Ralph's on several occasions) and dine out regularly at the most expensive restaurants. Shopping trips to London could be on a weekly basis when she would indulge in whatever designer creations appealed to her, while holidays to exotic and far-off destinations were also essential.

Insidious ideas sprang to mind. She knew what Kieran intended to cook for the main course – boeuf bourgignon – which would disguise other ingredients that could be added. *Don't be ridiculous*, Marina told herself. *You can't possibly do anything like that*, but nevertheless she started to work out a plan.

A week later, Isabel smiled politely, masking her surprise as she shook hands with Kieran. For some reason she had expected him to resemble his uncle: thickset and overpowering. Instead, she was greeted by a slim, quietly-spoken man whom she guessed to be about thirty.

She quickly noted his wavy black hair, grey eyes and smiled when he apologised for his casual appearance – smart open-necked shirt and dark blue trousers; he was cooking the meal. She was then introduced to a tall, well-built man, probably middle-aged, called Stefan Baumgarten and his wife; a tall, thin woman called Belinda; and finally, Marina, Kieran's partner, an attractive young woman.

During the course of the evening, Isabel learnt that Stefan's parents had moved to England in 1959, that he and Belinda had spent many enjoyable holidays in Austria and often visited the village where his grandfather had lived. 'Stefan is the general manager at one of the best hotels in Bristol,' said Belinda and after naming this, added, 'and Kieran is the restaurant manager there.'

This led to an interesting conversation as Marina recounted amusing incidents from her days as a courier when, together with a coachload of holidaymakers, she visited many European countries. It was on these occasions that she had received many compliments on her fluency in French, German and Italian. When not travelling, she had used her knowledge of the geography, culture and cuisine of these countries to become a travel writer. Currently, she was working for an escort agency where she was often called upon to accompany groups of European businessmen to places of interest in and around Bristol.

'You've also been a standby air courier, haven't you?' said Kieran.

'Couldn't that lead to complications?' enquired Duncan.

'I didn't have any problems. I only did it for two years,' and seeing Duncan's interest, Marina enlarged, 'anyone over eighteen and in good health can do this. Nationality is unimportant; you don't have to be the same nationality as the airline used.'

'Did you handle any of these packages yourself?' enquired Stefan.

'No. Usually company representatives at the departure and destination airports load and unload whatever needs accompanying, but the courier has to wait for customs to clear the items.'

'Weren't you worried that you could be accompanying suspicious packages or parcels?' asked Belinda.

'No. On each occasion that I travelled it was always for the same reput—'

'Darling, what about the pudding?' interrupted Kieran and as Marina carried the plates from the main course into the kitchen, 'I'm sorry about that.'

The remainder of the evening passed swiftly and Isabel was glad that no reference was made to Ralph's death or Leo's biography. It was as she said goodnight to their hosts that Isabel felt a strange pain in her stomach but said nothing. A few minutes later, she was home and was grateful for Duncan's hand on her arm as they walked the short distance to the front door when he took the key from her, inserted this and, at the same time, asked, 'Are you feeling all right? You haven't spoken since we left.'

'Just tired, I'll be fine by the morning.'

Slowly, Isabel made her way upstairs and with fumbling fingers undressed, not bothering that her clothes fell in an untidy heap, and climbed into bed.

But as she lay down, the pain began again, this time much worse, then with an effort she pushed the bedclothes aside and stumbled into the bathroom, just in time!

It was after she had been violently sick three times, but still felt terribly ill, that Isabel realised she should call Elspeth – they both slept with their doors ajar – but couldn't find the strength. Fortunately, her door was pushed open and Elspeth hurried in.

'What's happened? Are you ill?'

'I . . .' Isabel almost fell out of bed, moving awkwardly towards the bathroom and had barely reached it when she was violently sick again and collapsed.

'Oh my God!' gasped Elspeth, pulling Isabel back in the bedroom, and wiping her face with a cool flannel.

She quickly noted that while her pulse was weak, Isabel had a very high temperature. Placing her friend in such a position that she wouldn't choke if she was sick again, Elspeth dashed back to her room for her mobile, dialled for an ambulance and, after checking that Isabel was still conscious, phoned Dr Beresford and told him what she had done.

'I don't like the sound of it. It doesn't sound like an ordinary case of food poisoning,' said Dr Beresford. 'I'll go straight to the hospital.'

'Where did Isabel go this evening? What did she eat?' asked the doctor some time later. Isabel was now in a side ward, on a saline drip, weak and exhausted.

'She and Duncan were invited to a small dinner party given by Kieran O'Brien, Leo's nephew, but I've no idea what they ate.' As she said this, Elspeth gasped. 'I wonder if Duncan's all right? Shall I phone him?' and when the doctor nodded, reached into her bag for her mobile.

Although it was two o'clock in the morning, Duncan's voice was brisk as he demanded, 'Who's that? What's happened?' and while Elspeth was still explaining, 'Is she conscious? Do you want me to come to the hospital?'

At this, Elspeth handed her mobile to the doctor who said, 'I'm glad to hear you haven't been sick; however, can you tell me what you ate this evening?'

After writing for a few seconds, the doctor read this out and asked, 'Is Isabel allergic to any of this?'

'No, she usually enjoys spicy dishes and sauces.'

Elspeth paused. 'Duncan only said avocado and prawns, no mention of sauce but there probably was one, and Isabel usually enjoys boeuf bourgignon.' Then, wrinkling her nose in distaste, Elspeth continued, 'The ambulance came so quickly I couldn't clean the bathroom. Poor Isabel didn't reach the toilet the last time she was sick.'

'That's good; I'd like to know what caused this. Whatever it was didn't affect Duncan,' and without pausing, the doctor asked, 'would you like a lift home?'

'Thank you.'

Detective Sergeant Tom Small had ignored the ringing of the inspector's phone but now looked up from his computer screen as Inspector Kershaw exclaimed, 'Isabel McGuire's in hospital!' and then, 'Would you mind repeating that, Dr Beresford?'

Tom continued to watch the inspector's changing expressions and his frantic scribbling, unable to comprehend the gist of the one-sided conversation. At last, Kershaw replaced the receiver and said, 'You probably understood some of that; however, thanks to Elspeth's promptness, Isabel was rushed into hospital late last night with food poisoning. At least that's what

Beresford thought at the time – he was very worried about her. Now he's waiting for the results of some tests as to what caused her to be so violently ill.'

'Hang on a minute, sir. Could you clarify some of that?'

'Good idea. It will help me to clear my mind before deciding what to do,' and seeing Tom's puzzled expression, Kershaw enlarged, 'when Isabel collapsed after being so sick, Elspeth rang for the ambulance and then the doctor, who went directly to the hospital. Sometime later, Elspeth told Beresford that Isabel and Duncan had been invited to dinner by Kieran O'Brien, Adare's nephew.'

'My God! That couldn't have been a coin…' Kershaw ignored this interruption and continued. 'The doctor learnt from Duncan, who had not been sick, that the other guests were a couple called Baumgarten.'

'Are they all right?'

'They might have been sick at home, but no one else was admitted to hospital.'

'Was something added to Isabel's food? What did they eat? Who did the cooking? What caused…?'

Tom stopped abruptly when Kershaw told him, 'Dr Beresford will phone as soon as he receives the results.'

'I can't stay here. I'm not really ill,' protested Isabel when Elspeth visited her later that afternoon.

'Dr Beresford insists. I don't think you realise how ill you were last night; you're still very weak.'

Elspeth looked at Isabel and tried to keep her voice light. 'Relax and try to sleep. Then, if you feel up to it, Duncan would like to see you, possibly this evening, just for a few minutes.'

'Is he all right? I wonder if the other guests—'

'He's fine,' interrupted Elspeth, for some reason recalling that the smell in Isabel's bathroom had been disgusting even that morning, in spite of disinfectant, air freshener and leaving the window wide open. She had been surprised that Dr Beresford had wanted a sample analysed but supposed this happened after someone had been so ill. As she bent to kiss Isabel's cheek, Elspeth noticed her waxy complexion and clammy hands and was glad when a nurse appeared, studied Isabel as she lay back against the pillows and nodded approvingly.

'That's right, my dear. You lie there comfortably and try to sleep.'

As she accompanied Elspeth into the corridor, the nurse resumed, 'I'm glad to see Mrs McGuire is improving. The night team were very worried about her and wondered if anyone else was going to be brought in.' Then glancing at Elspeth, 'You don't look too good. Did you eat the same thing?'

'No, I wasn't invited. It's just that I didn't sleep. I was worried about Isabel.'

'There's no need for you to do that now. You can rest assured that we'll take great care of her.'

'I wonder if Kieran and Marina or the Baumgartens were sick,' said Duncan as he sat facing Elspeth across the kitchen table. He had promised to call in on his way home from the hospital and had been relieved to see that Isabel did not look as bad as Elspeth had described, and was not surprised when Isabel told him that her tummy felt extremely sore.

'I was really grateful when Dr Beresford arrived at the hospital so quickly. He was very concerned about Isabel and I'm glad he's keeping her in hospital until tomorrow, maybe Thursday.'

'So am I.' Duncan flicked through the telephone directory. 'I think Kieran should be—'

'No,' interrupted Elspeth. 'I was going to do that this morning but Dr Beresford told me not to do anything. He's waiting for the results of the tests and said if there was anything untoward he would take the appropriate steps.'

'That sounds ominous.'

9

It was late afternoon when Inspector Kershaw answered the phone and his expression immediately became sombre as he asked, 'Could you repeat that?' Detective Sergeant Small watched as the inspector listened and nodded, at the same time muttering to himself, then eventually Kershaw asked, 'Do you know what caused this, where it came from?' and finally, 'could Isabel have died?'

Bursting with curiosity, Tom struggled to remain patient as Kershaw asked more pertinent questions and finally said, 'Let me know as soon as you hear, please. However, how long do you propose to keep Isabel in hospital?'

'What—' began Tom.

But he was quickly silenced by Kershaw saying, 'Time for us to see Kieran O'Brien and the Baumgartens.' However, as they set off for Henleaze, Tom learnt that some type of berry had been added to Isabel's main course, but further tests were being carried out. Dr Beresford would advise the chief inspector as soon as he heard the results.

Kieran's displeasure was obvious as he answered the front door and demanded, 'What d'you want?'

'Police' said Kershaw as he and Tom quickly produced their warrant cards. 'We'd like to ask you a few questions about the dinner party you gave on Monday evening.'

'Which is nothing to do with you.'

'But it could be, especially as one of your guests was rushed into hospital and…'

'What!' exclaimed a female voice and an attractive brunette appeared behind Kieran. 'You can't keep these police officers standing on the doorstep,' she said, addressing Kershaw. 'Please come in.' Once the front door was closed and they were ushered into a medium-sized, sparsely furnished lounge she asked, 'What happened?' then, seeing Kershaw's raised eyebrows, 'I'm Marina Bushell, Kieran's partner. Can I offer you some tea or coffee?'

'Is it Belinda or Stefan?' enquired Kieran a few moments later when the two detectives were seated. 'I haven't seen either of them in the garden.'

Kershaw knew that their gardens backed onto each other and noted the concern in his voice. 'No, it was Mrs McGuire…'

'Was?' interrupted Kieran.

'You don't mean she's dead!' This came from Marina whose voice was almost a whisper.

Kershaw noticed that Kieran, standing almost rigid, remained silent and was glad when Tom said, 'Haven't you anything else to say, Mr O'Brien? Mrs McGuire was a guest in your house, ate your food…'

'Are you insinuating there was something wrong with it? I've had friends to dinner before, cooked the same dish and everyone was fine.' Then glancing at Marina, 'That was when I lived in a tiny flat and before I knew you. No one was ever ill.'

'Don't look at me like that,' said Marina. 'You bought the food and cooked the meal,' then turning to the inspector, 'I wasn't allowed in the kitchen. I spent some time in the utility room where I did a small flower arrangement and then laid the table.'

'You enjoy cooking, Mr O'Brien?' queried Kershaw then, without pausing, 'have a look in the kitchen, Sergeant.'

'You can't do that,' protested Kieran. 'It's… it's an infringement of our privacy. You need a search warrant.'

'Which could easily be obtained. Mrs McGuire almost died and is still seriously ill as a result of food poisoning.' Kershaw could see that Kieran was now looking worried but, in spite of this, reminded him, 'From food eaten in your house.'

As Marina led Tom into the hall and towards the kitchen, Kershaw resumed, catching Kieran unawares,

'Why didn't you contribute something towards Leo Adare's biography? There must have been some amusing anecdotes from when you were a small boy. After all, he is your uncle…'

'He certainly didn't behave like one. There was no avuncular affection,' expostulated Kieran. 'We hardly ever saw him, even after my father pushed off. You would have thought that my mother being his only sister, he would have checked to find out how she was coping. And on the occasions that he did call, he wasn't interested in us. It was all about him and now he's apparently full of this biography. It's bloody ridiculous, quite unnecessary and I doubt that he wants to publicise his messy affairs with young men. But what's this all about? Why are you interested in him?'

'It's strange that Ralph McGuire died under suspicious circumstances, enquiries are still being made, now that Isabel is now very ill.'

'I agree and I'm very sorry about Mrs McGuire. However, as far as the meal I prepared and cooked is concerned, I can't think of any reason why this happened.' Kieran now looked and sounded worried. 'I'm always very careful when shopping, make sure that no ingredients are past their sell-by date. Everything I bought was fresh. It might have been something she ate for breakfast or lunch. She was fine when she left…'

Kieran broke off as Tom reappeared and then Kershaw said quickly, 'Thank you, Mr O'Brien. If you're leaving Bristol for any reason, please advise me of your destination.'

The Baumgartens had not been mentioned, and in the short time it took Tom to drive round to their house, Kershaw learnt that the search, although thorough, had been futile. 'There was sufficient time for any traces, or any remaining substances, to be removed,' commented Kershaw.

Belinda Baumgarten's squeal brought Stefan hurrying to the front door where he gazed at Kershaw with curiosity. 'How can we help you, Inspector?'

'By answering a few questions about the dinner party that you attended on Monday.'

'Of course. Come in, please.' Stefan glanced at Belinda then, standing aside, ushered the two detectives into a lounge the same size as Kieran's but more expensively decorated and furnished. Declining the offer of tea, coffee or anything stronger, Kershaw did not waste any time, noting the Baumgartens' genuine concern that Isabel had been so ill.

'It's strange that she was the only person who was ill; we all ate the same thing. We enjoyed our meal and didn't suffer any side effects,' volunteered Stefan.

'Perhaps she was allergic to something?' hazarded Belinda and gazed at Kershaw open-mouthed when she learnt that a toxic substance had been added to Isabel's main course.

'I don't believe it! Marina and Kieran seem a nice couple, why should either of them do such a terrible thing?' Stefan removed his glasses and rubbed his eyes. 'Wait a minute. I've just remembered there was someone in the kitchen with Kieran when we arrived. We were standing just inside the lounge with our drinks when I saw this young man walk through the hall and let himself out.'

Kershaw knew that Stefan Baumgarten was general manager of a large hotel near the centre and that Kieran also worked there, and now asked, 'Have you seen this young man before?'

'No, but I would certainly know him again. He's tall with spiky, jet black hair. There seemed to be something familiar about him. I'm certain I've seen him before but I can't think where.'

'Thank you, Mr Baumgarten. That's very helpful.'

Kershaw had noticed that the prints on the walls were of an Austrian village and now asked, 'Do you return to Austria very often?'

'Yes,' and following Kershaw's gaze, Stefan told him, 'that's the village where my grandfather lived. My parents lived in Vienna until we came to England in 1959, but I still have some relatives living in that village. We usually spend some time with them, also in Salzburg and Vienna. Belinda likes the shops.'

'So you buy Austrian clothes when you're there?'

'Sometimes. Although the Loden coats and suits are expensive, they last for years.'

Tom had listened to this brief exchange with interest and, as soon as they were outside, he asked, 'Surely you don't think Stefan…'

'It's early days. Let's go back and see O'Brien. It's interesting that they both work at the same hotel, Baumgarten having been there for years and he is now the general manager while O'Brien is the restaurant manager. However, I want to know more about this young man who was in the kitchen when dinner was being prepared.'

Ten minutes later, after a brief but unsatisfactory conversation, Tom was driving back to the station while Kershaw thought about what was said. They had learnt that the caller, Zak Amory, had been Leo Adare's previous lover but was now living in Bristol and currently appearing at the Old Vic. 'So that's why I know his name,' muttered Kershaw.

At first, Kieran had protested. It was none of their business, then he grudgingly imparted this information, stating that he had first met Zak when he dined at the hotel. 'Zak had been offered his first role at the Old Vic that morning and, although it meant dining alone, had decided to celebrate. We had a few drinks in a nearby pub after I'd finished, and have been friends ever since,' said Kieran. He added that they enjoyed each other's company and, because they both worked in the evenings, they sometimes met for a game of squash in the afternoon, and reluctantly gave the inspector Zak's address.

'It's possible Ralph's death and Isabel's poisoning are connected with Adare's biography,' mused Kershaw.

'Kieran certainly has no time for his uncle, doesn't approve of the biography, resents the publicity it will create and it's quite likely that Zak feels the same. Obviously, we can't see him now, but we'll call on him in the morning.'

Later that evening, when Belinda was engrossed in a library book, Stefan considered it was strange that Isabel McGuire had been invited to Kieran's dinner party. He knew that she and Duncan Sinclair were now working on the biography of Leo Adare and was glad that this, and Ralph's death, had not been discussed.

Stefan's dislike of Leo began a long time ago and his thoughts now turned to his cousin, Manfred. With only six months difference in age, they had spent a lot of time together, become very close and were both upset when, in 1959, Stefan's parents moved to England. They had kept in touch. Stefan had visited Vienna every year while Manfred came to England. Later, when Manfred was almost twenty-two, Stefan had noticed a change in his cousin and had been distressed to learn that Manfred was suffering from a debilitating illness. He had been seen by physicians, diagnostics and specialists, but the outlook was grim. There was no known cure and Manfred's life expectancy was three years. However, Helmut and Olga had been advised that there was a clinic in Switzerland where Manfred could receive treatment which might relieve his pain and discomfort.

Stefan recalled his amazement that his Uncle Helmut did not want Manfred's illness to be known by friends or business associates and had expressed his disapproval of the suggestion that Leo Adare (who had already been mistaken for Manfred) should stand in while Manfred received this treatment. On his annual visit, he learnt from his uncle that Leo was doing well, but his Aunt Olga confided that Leo's manner towards her was too familiar and had been grateful for Stefan's support when Manfred died. Leo had left the country immediately, without a word of sympathy or compassion, when Stefan's uncle and aunt had been disgusted by Leo's callousness.

Stefan smiled as he remembered the first time he had met Belinda. He had been working in reception in a London hotel while she worked in one of the large departmental stores, and they had married eighteen months later.

Securing the position of head receptionist at the hotel of which he was now general manager had been the beginning of an interesting and successful career. Over the years he had been in charge of various departments, and his enthusiasm and foresight had been recognised when the property adjacent to the hotel was purchased and converted to conference rooms and luxury suites. The general manager at that time had noted his ideas for the conversion and sent him to Europe to ascertain what was being offered to affluent businessmen and tourists. He had returned with his head and notebook full of what he had seen and learnt and was thrilled to be included in the meetings with the architects and interior designers. That was some time ago, and the whole hotel had been redecorated and refurbished many times and, no matter which department he had been working in, or in charge of, he was always included in the discussions regarding this. He had found his time as personnel manager somewhat arduous but gradually adjusted to this, getting to know the different members of staff, enjoying dealing with all the events that the hotel was now able to cater for – banquets, small or large dinner parties, conferences, and weddings. He had also been interested to see the hotel grow. Another building had been acquired and converted, bedrooms had been enlarged to become spacious suites that were in constant demand. A brasserie, leisure centre and beauty salon had been added, while the kitchen was completely reorganised and re-equipped.

As the years passed he had noted that Leo had become more successful but was still trailing those with household names. Stefan recalled the afternoon Kieran told him that Leo Adare was his uncle. Kieran and his partner Marina had moved into the house whose garden backed on to theirs, five years ago. They had been working in their respective gardens, pausing to comment that it was too hot to do much, when he said that he and Belinda were going to the theatre that night. Kieran had spoken about his mother and Leo's heartless attitude when his father had walked out. Leo could have helped out financially, even on a temporary basis, but he didn't, hence Kieran's intense dislike of his uncle.

10

'Good morning, Inspector, Sergeant. Please come in.' Zak Amory stood in the narrow hallway and indicated an open door. 'I hope you'll excuse the untidiness. I usually rush off to the theatre and certainly don't feel like clearing up when I come home.' Zak picked up papers and magazines from two easy chairs, still talking. 'Kieran left a message that you would be calling on me.'

Kershaw suppressed a smile at Zak's exuberance, Tom's bewildered expression and the small but colourful room. Full-length midnight blue curtains fell on either side of a long, narrow window, contrasting against the pale turquoise wall, but matching the opposite wall. A worn two-seater settee was pushed against this, and a table, littered with pages of a manuscript, stood in front of the window. Pushing these aside, Zak added his pile of papers and said, 'I'm sorry that the settee and the chairs aren't very comfortable, but please sit down and tell me how I can help you.'

Kershaw chose a shabby easy chair and looked at

the young actor who had seated himself, cross-legged, on the floor. In his bright green t-shirt, which almost matched his eyes, and baggy red shorts, Zak looked like a teenager, certainly not twenty-five. 'I understand you called on Kieran O'Brien Monday evening. How long did you stay and were you in the kitchen all the time?'

Zak's green eyes glittered. 'Ah, that was the evening of the dinner party. I was only there for a few minutes before going to the theatre. I know it's not on my way but I often do that. I knew Kieran was having a dinner party – he was cooking boeuf bourgignon and it smelt delicious. He offered me a drink but I didn't have one.'

'What was he actually doing while you were there? Did you see him or Marina add anything to it?'

'He was putting the final touches to the first course, avocado and prawns, which looked very appetising.'

'What was Marina doing?' enquired Tom, moving cautiously on an unsteady straight-backed chair.

'Fiddling around with flowers.' Zak grinned mischievously. 'She called it "flower arranging" when she brought it through the kitchen. It didn't look all that special. We only exchanged a few words when she went back to the utility room to tidy up. Then, when their neighbours arrived, she joined them in the lounge.'

Although Kershaw knew Isabel and Duncan arrived after Zak had left, he asked, 'Did Mrs McGuire arrive while you were there?'

'No, and if you're wondering if I was in the kitchen

alone, yes, but only for a few seconds while Kieran and Marina greeted their neighbours.' Zak looked from Kershaw to Tom and back again. 'But I didn't touch anything; how was I to know which first course would be placed in front of Mrs McGuire? In any case, I don't know anything about poisons and certainly wouldn't know how to obtain them.' Zak broke off. 'I'm sorry, I've been very remiss. Would you like a coffee? It'll have to be instant, while I tell you about myself, which I'm sure you want to know.'

'Thank you; that would be very acceptable.' Kershaw then learnt that Zak's parents had split up when he was fifteen. His father, remarried with a young family, now lived in Yorkshire while his mother was a successful businesswoman in London. His maternal grandmother, who was still in Plymouth where he was born, phoned him at least twice a week and was genuinely interested in his career and glad he had moved to Bristol, and he was no longer associated with Leo Adare.

'I know he was very kind to me – I learnt a lot from him. He persuaded the casting director to give me a minor role in which I only spoke about five sentences, but that didn't prevent him from being an arrogant and selfish bastard.'

Kershaw refrained from saying he thought the same and then Zak resumed, 'Although Kieran has told me I'm always welcome at their place, I don't want to intrude. And now, thanks to a reasonable and regular wage, and help from Grandma, I've a new motorbike.

I can visit her on a regular basis and explore the countryside around and beyond Bristol. It's wonderful!'

On hearing this, Tom looked up, enquired about the make and capabilities and grinned, 'Sounds great but I doubt if my girlfriend would appreciate it.'

'I don't have to worry about things like that.'

'We don't have much choice about who poisoned Isabel,' said Tom as they reached the pavement. 'It must be Kieran or Marina and it was probably in the boeuf bourgignon. The first two people to be served were the ladies, and Kieran didn't indicate which was for Belinda or Isabel. Marina brought the plates in from the kitchen, set down Belinda's and then Isabel's.'

Kershaw nodded. 'I must say Kieran is very competent. He told us the ingredients and how it was cooked without any hesitation. It's obviously a dish he's cooked on several occasions but, in spite of that, he's very worried about what happened.'

'I expect Mrs Baumgarten has been thinking she had a lucky escape,' said Tom. 'But why should Kieran or Marina want to harm Isabel, who was a complete stranger?'

'That's something else for us to find out.'

'Oh, I'm so glad to see you!' exclaimed Elspeth as she hugged Isabel.

'And I'm pleased to be home,' said Isabel, turning to smile at Duncan who had just brought her from the hospital.

'Go into the lounge, put your feet up and we'll all have a cup of tea,' said Elspeth.

'What on earth!' gasped Isabel as she stood in the doorway, her gaze focused on a large, colourful flower arrangement.

Duncan grinned and said, 'They're from Hugo with instructions that you're to take it easy for the rest of the week. Dr Beresford is going to look in this evening.'

'Surely that's unnecessary. I'm home and feeling fine.' Isabel examined the carnations then the delicate petals of the alstroemerias, unaware of Elspeth and Duncan's expressions, that they were both concerned that Detective Inspector Kershaw had been informed.

'I'm sorry to disturb you, Mrs McGuire, but I would like to question you about Adare's biography.' It was Thursday afternoon and Kershaw had phoned that morning to enquire if it was convenient for him to call and see her.

'Surely this isn't in any way connected with Ralph's death?' queried Duncan, whose presence had been requested.

'What can you tell me about Zak Amory?' and noting their exchanged glances, 'Have you come across his name?' Although he had met the young actor the previous morning and found him to be pleasant and informative, Kershaw was still interested to learn more about him.

'No. Who is he and how do you know about him?' asked Isabel.

'He's a young actor. He was Leo's protégé,' and aware of Isabel's curious expression, 'yes, he did have a relationship with Leo until it was abruptly terminated. Zak has been living in Bristol for approximately two years and is currently appearing at the Old Vic.'

'How do you know all this?' asked Duncan while Isabel looked on, speechless.

'He's a friend of Kieran's. Zak was at the house before the dinner party. He left just before you arrived.'

Isabel shook her head. 'I'm sorry, but I don't see where this is leading.'

Kershaw recalled his conversation with the three actresses after Ralph's funeral. 'I'm surprised that when you spoke to Leo's dresser you weren't told about him, or the relationship.'

'He certainly didn't mention anyone. In fact, he didn't have much to say. He didn't want to contribute.'

'Perhaps if he didn't have anything amusing or favourable to say he thought it better to say nothing. He didn't want to upset Adare, possibly lose his job,' ventured Duncan. Then turning to Isabel, 'Did anyone, even Adare himself, ever mention any women?'

'Not to me. He may have spoken to Ralph, but there weren't any notes on girlfriends or mistresses.'

Isabel turned back to Kershaw. 'Why are you so interested in this young actor?'

'Apparently, he was very upset when Leo told him to get out, was jealous of his successor – a virile Jamaican, who is a portrait artist, and he doesn't approve of Leo's biography. Neither does Kieran O'Brien.'

Isabel looked at Duncan and then back to Kershaw. 'What's this got to do with me, or rather the biography? We still don't know,' and with an apologetic glance at the inspector, 'the police haven't found out who the mysterious caller was, and it now turns out that Amory and O'Brien were together before the dinner party.'

'Enquiries are—'

'If they're both so against this biography – and I don't see why they are so bothered, neither of them are mentioned – why wait until now, when it's nearly finished?' interrupted Isabel. 'Why didn't they tell Leo at the beginning?'

'Perhaps they did and, knowing of Adare's bad temper, were told to mind their own business,' offered Duncan. Then, looking at Kershaw again, 'Was that the only reason for your visit?'

'Yes; however, I would like to know more about Leo Adare, if the contents of the biography are in any way controversial?'

It was some time later. Kershaw had departed, satisfied with the answer to his last question, when Elspeth said, 'I can't really believe that the inspector thinks Ralph's death and your food poisoning are connected with this damn biography. If it's going to cause any more trouble why don't you abandon it?'

'I wouldn't want to do that; a lot of research and hard work has gone into it already. I just don't understand why Kieran and Zak are so against it. There's no mention of Zak or any of his predecessors, and there probably were some.' Isabel paused but only for a moment. 'It's not as though it refers to industrial espionage, political sleaze or...' Isabel stopped abruptly.

'What's bothering you?' asked Duncan.

'I'm just going to check on something before I say anything else.'

Ten minutes elapsed, with Elspeth and Duncan both deep in thought, then Isabel burst back into the lounge, 'I was right. There is a gap.'

'What are you talking about?' asked Duncan while Elspeth nodded but said nothing.

'There's no mention, no reviews or anything of what he was doing from the time he was twenty-two to twenty-five. That's a three-year gap.'

'Perhaps he was abroad touring,' suggested Duncan.

'In which case he would have wanted it included,' said Isabel. 'What do you think, Elspeth?'

'I noticed there was something missing when I read the completed chapters.'

'The aunts must have realised there was nothing in the albums for that period. Anyhow, I'm going to fetch them.'

'There's nothing here for the relevant years,' said Duncan some time later as he closed the first album and placed it on a nearby table. Then, after picking up another album and studying a few pages, 'However, the aunts have made a good job of these.'

'Yes, but I must return them. I'll drive down and see the aunts next week, and hopefully learn where Leo was at that time.' Isabel drank her tea, ate the slice of cake and went off to ring Emily O'Brien. Returning to the lounge a few minutes later, she said, 'I asked if there is anything else that should be included and they're both going to think about it. I'm seeing them next Tuesday so that gives them the weekend to reminisce. There's been nothing about ill health, so I'll check the previous chapter.'

'A three-year gap,' repeated Duncan. 'It's almost like a prison sentence,' and looking across at Isabel and Elspeth, 'but it couldn't have been that, could it?'

'With his proclivity for younger men it makes

one wonder if he was involved with very young boys,' offered Elspeth.

'That would have been damn stupid,' muttered Duncan.

'Suppose… just suppose he was asked to stand in for someone important whom he resembled?' Isabel could see Elspeth and Duncan were regarding her as though she had two heads but this didn't stop her. 'I mean to say, during the war or even in times of crisis, doubles or lookalikes of notable personalities were often sent to dangerous areas or assignments. We all know actors have long spells "resting". This could have been one of those periods, and knowing Leo's love of importance and ostentation, he could have jumped at this opportunity.'

'But who did he stand in for, and for three years?' queried Duncan. 'No, I'm afraid your imagination is running away with you. What do you think, Elspeth?'

'Strange things do happen. You read about these "sleepers" who are suddenly called in, asked to go abroad, act as undercover agents.'

'Now I've heard the lot!' exclaimed Duncan. 'Are you telling me Adare was approached by a dissident party in his student days and they suddenly called on him?' Duncan paused and grinned at Isabel. 'You could be wasting your time and talent on biographies. With ideas like these, why don't the two of you put your heads together? I'm sure you could come up with a fantastic plot and, with your connections, anything you wrote would be a bestseller.'

'Why didn't I think of that?' Elspeth grinned at Isabel. 'There's something in Duncan's suggestion; it's certainly worth thinking about.'

'Let's get this biography finished. I must say I'm surprised Ralph didn't notice the gap when he discussed the outline with Leo.' Isabel stood up. 'I'm going to look through his original notes.'

Detective Inspector Kershaw muttered to himself. He had just returned to the station after visiting Isabel and was frustrated that the unknown caller had not yet been found. Detective Sergeant Small's enquiries at the various shops that hired out fancy dress costumes and other outfits had been futile, while Stefan Baumgarten had repeated that he and Belinda had driven down to Minehead for the day. Stefan also stated that he had never lent any of his Austrian clothes to anyone, even for use by the amateur dramatic society to which Belinda belonged.

The house-to-house enquiries had resulted in only Mr Gresham's observation. Kershaw considered that it was a ridiculous situation and knew that his frustration was aggravated by the superintendent's criticism that his team were dragging their heels – this simply wasn't true!

Once again he considered the idea that Leo's biography was the cause of the trouble. Ralph was dead.

If Isabel had died as a result of the food poisoning, would Duncan have carried on with it? Hugo Forrester had told him that Adare definitely wanted it completed. Leo was sorry about Ralph's death – this had been inevitable, but he knew that Isabel was capable of completing this.

Leo had been staying in his cottage at Wedmore the previous Sunday and, after stating that a visit from Kershaw was unnecessary, eventually agreed to see him.

The countryside had looked at its best, the cottage on the outskirts of the village, picturesque, and Dominic, the lithe Jamaican who had opened the front door, had shown him into a tastefully furnished living room and left them alone.

Adare had boasted of his success, that his biography would be well-received by his fans and, unaware that he was doing so, Kershaw muttered, 'Arrogant bastard!' when Tom queried, 'What's the matter? Can I do anything?'

'It's this damn biography that keeps troubling me. Could it be connected with Ralph's death, Isabel's food poisoning?' and before Tom could reply, 'You read the completed chapters and notes for the remainder of the script. Was there anything that struck you as odd or so detrimental that the person concerned would take umbrage, or such drastic action?'

'No, but I did notice that in one place, when Leo was in his early twenties, it didn't follow on. One minute he was touring with a repertory company then the next he was appearing in a new play in Chichester. It didn't make sense, and yet it didn't seem important.'

Kershaw looked thoughtful. 'I wonder what length of time there was in between. Perhaps Leo was in some kind of trouble; in which case, he wouldn't want anyone to know,' and in the same breath, 'Isabel is very observant. I'm surprised she hasn't said anything.'

'Why should she? It's Ralph's death and her food poisoning that we're invest—'

'I know and unfortunately we're not making much progress,' interrupted Kershaw. 'We've checked and found nothing in Ralph's background, so it must be connected with the biography. I realise we've only just left, but what you said could be important. I'm going to ring Isabel. If it's a wild goose chase, that's too bad.'

Isabel answered on the study extension when Elspeth heard her exclaim, 'So your sergeant noticed it!' The conversation was brief and when she returned to the lounge, Isabel explained that Detective Sergeant Small had noticed that the contents of that particular chapter didn't follow on, and the inspector was curious as to whether anything untoward had occurred.

Meanwhile, Kershaw told Tom, 'Isabel is aware

of what you noticed and is waiting for a suitable opportunity to ask Hugo Forrester or, if necessary, Adare. She'll let me know if she learns anything of importance.'

'In the meantime, why would Kieran or Marina want to harm Isabel? Neither of them had ever met her before,' queried Tom.

11

'Are you really feeling better?' Isabel noted the genuine concern in Hugo's voice and after assuring him that she did, and had started work on the biography again, thanked him for the elaborate flower arrangement.

'They were all lovely but the alstroemerias are quite fantastic, strong stalks but very delicate petals and such lovely colours.'

'It's odd that you were the only person who was ill; in fact, I didn't realise you knew Leo's nephew, Kieran O'Brien.'

'I didn't and although you haven't asked, he didn't mention his uncle or the biography, maybe because there were other guests. A very pleasant couple: Stefan Baumgarten, he's Austrian and general manager at the same hotel where Kieran works, and his wife Belinda.'

Isabel had discussed the three-year gap again with Elspeth and Duncan and now asked, 'Did you know we haven't anything on Leo from the time he was twenty-two until he was twenty-five, and I can't find any reference to this in Ralph's original notes.'

'What are you talking about? This is the first I've heard about it. Leo assured me there was nothing untoward in his earlier years and Ralph didn't say anything.' And after a slight pause, 'Are you going to contact Leo about it?'

'Not yet. I'm returning the photograph albums to his two elderly aunts, who live in Sidmouth, tomorrow. It's possible they might know something.'

'Hugo doesn't know anything either?' queried Duncan a few minutes later.

'No.' Isabel's thoughts turned briefly to the fact that Kieran had not mentioned his uncle and decided that Duncan could contact him regarding his contribution to the biography. When this was first discussed, Leo had spoken about his two aunts – retired teachers and now very elderly – when Ralph had despatched her to Devon.

Isabel recalled how much she had enjoyed that day. It had been early spring and she had driven slowly through the countryside from Exeter to the coast. The two old ladies, both tall and thin, had been garrulous, each offering information about Leo's early interest in acting, his imitations of well-known actors, and produced albums of cuttings and photographs. They still avidly followed his career and were disappointed that Kieran had not shown any interest in acting or the theatre. Emily, the eldest, had volunteered that until three years ago they had attended Leo's first nights – he had always sent them tickets. However, they no longer travelled to London or anywhere else, but they always received a programme and short note, and naturally cut out all the reviews.

Duncan's voice cut into her thoughts. 'Do you feel up to driving that far?'

'I'll be fine and this will give me an opportunity to return their hospitality. Emily is going to book a table at one of the hotels on the esplanade.'

It was later that day that Duncan surprised Isabel by asking, 'Do you intend to stay on in this house?'

'I hadn't really thought about it but yes, I suppose so. Why do you ask?'

'It's a big house for the two of you and, without being rude, these old houses can be expensive to maintain.'

'Yes, I had realised that. However, at the moment we should concentrate on completing this biography.'

'A day away will probably stimulate you,' said Duncan. 'I'll arrange to see Kieran and find out if he's prepared to make a contribution, and collate all my notes.'

Duncan was right, thought Isabel late the following afternoon as she waved goodbye to the two aunts and headed back to Exeter. She had enjoyed the drive down to Sidmouth and had been warmly welcomed by the two ladies who had been eager to chat about Leo, his schooldays and even then, his dreams of being a famous actor. The lunch had been delicious and sustaining when she had learnt that they both did voluntary work for different charities, were keen churchgoers and involved in various church activities.

It was as they studied the sweet menu that she mentioned dinner with Kieran and Marina and Emily said, 'Do you know, we've only seen him twice since his mother died.' Immediately, Isabel realised that Leo had never spoken of a sister and noticed that the two lined faces had become sad, both murmuring, 'Poor Maeve.'

It was Dorothy who elaborated. 'She was such a pretty girl, had a lovely voice but her husband was a brute. He wouldn't allow her to visit us – that was long before we came down here, but she kept in touch when he left her. In spite of his constant bullying, she was still an attractive young woman, determined to make a new life for herself and Kieran. It was a great pity Leo wasn't more supportive; he didn't even attend her funeral. We were really disgusted; it wasn't as though he was on tour.'

At this point, Emily intervened. 'Maeve died in

a multiple car crash,' and added, 'if Kieran had any aspirations to follow in his uncle's footsteps, Leo's behaviour must have destroyed them.'

Inevitably, the conversation returned to Leo when both aunts agreed that they had thought it strange that there had been nothing between him touring with a repertory company and then appearing in a well-known play in Chichester. Then, to Isabel's surprise, they simultaneously commented on his preference for male partners. 'But we've never seen a photo of him with any of them,' volunteered Emily.

'Has he ever spoken about his personal life, spoken of one particular person?' asked Isabel.

'No.'

As she approached Exeter, Isabel decided to avoid the motorway and enjoy more of the countryside, villages and small towns. At the same time, she recalled the tears in Emily's eyes and Dorothy's concern when they learnt of Ralph's death and was glad she had not told them that she had been rushed to hospital, and that the police were making enquiries.

'I'm pleased to see you enjoying your food again,' said Elspeth that evening as she observed Isabel's clean plate.

'After a substantial lunch, quiche and salad was ideal.' Isabel had just summarised what she had learnt from the two aunts, their comments about Leo, Kieran and Maeve, and was not surprised when Elspeth said, 'Leo doesn't come out of this as a very caring person. Even though he didn't like or approve of Maeve's husband, he could have shown some affection and consideration when she was left to bring up Kieran on her own.'

'That's what I thought. In fact, right from the beginning, Leo has appeared as arrogant. He told us very little about his parents and refused Ralph's suggestion that we needed more information about them. I tried to reason with Ralph about it, told him that the aunts had spoken about Leo's parents when he said, quite vehemently, that I should mind my own business and ignore all that. I also pointed out the lack of information about Leo's childhood, schooldays and adolescence, but he was adamant that what had been written was sufficient for Leo's fans. I'm sure Ralph knew nothing about Maeve; there was nothing in any of his notes about Leo having a sister. It's as though Leo was ashamed of her; yet, according to the aunts, Maeve was a pretty child with a lovely voice.'

'Perhaps he was jealous,' offered Elspeth.

'Although I'd met Kieran, I didn't really think of his mother as being Leo's sister until today, and then I was disgusted at what I learnt.'

'I feel the same.' Elspeth stood up and looked

around the dining room. 'I realise this is a sudden change of subject; however, what are you going to do about the house?'

'Have you been talking to Duncan?' and when Elspeth shook her head, 'He asked me the same question and my answer is I don't know. But why do you ask?'

'I realise I've lived here most of my life, but it is rather big for the two of us.'

'That was Duncan's comment, and you're both right. He also mentioned the maintenance of a house this age and size. I know it's something I'll have to think about, with your help and advice, but not until we've finished Leo's biography. I certainly couldn't face a move until then and before starting work on something new.' Isabel had been surprised that in spite of Ralph's illness and his death she had received several enquiries to write more biographies.

On her return from Sidmouth, Isabel had found a message from Duncan. There had been requests from a well-known local sportsman and an elderly local politician, and she now looked around the large dining room. They had all discussed redecorating this. Ralph had reluctantly agreed that the room did look shabby, but before they could decide on a colour scheme or choose wallpaper, Ralph's symptoms had worsened and the idea had been forgotten. At the same time, she had hoped to dispense with the heavy old-fashioned table, chairs and matching sideboard which, like the house, Ralph had inherited from his parents. Isabel quickly decided that a four bedroom house was really unnecessary. Joanna's brief stay after Ralph's death had been the first time the spare room had been used for many years and, without thinking, voiced her thoughts. 'Heaven only knows what's up in the attic.'

'Fortunately, not much – suitcases and two large trunks.' Elspeth looked at Isabel with concern. 'Don't even think about moving. There's plenty of time.'

'I won't, but there is something we must do. Look out the books that Ralph left to the university library.' A codicil to this effect had been made as Ralph's illness progressed and Peter Hoskins, the solicitor, had advised the master of the university of this bequest.

Meanwhile, Leo Adare was stretched out on an elegant chaise longue, his grey eyes glinting as he appraised the slim, athletic body of Dominic, his young Jamaican lover, and in his well-known stage voice he said, 'Shall we go to Venice next week?'

Dominic grinned with delight. 'What a marvellous idea! I really enjoyed our previous visit but didn't think we would be returning so soon.' Dominic had cornered something of a niche market as a society painter and he resumed, 'I'm sure Lady Cumings will agree to postpone her sitting until the following week.'

'Of course she will. She's such a charming and

understanding person.' Leo knew many of the people whose portraits Dominic had painted. They had been together for nearly three years. Their relationship was still as passionate as when they first met, which was at an art exhibition, and Leo now said, 'Everything is booked, our flights and the same suite at the Cipriani.'

'Fantastic!' Dominic's eyes lit up with anticipation. 'I've seen Venice in the autumn and now I'll see it in the spring.'

Leo nodded. 'Yes, it should be lovely.'

'Vienna is another city I'd like to visit. Perhaps we could go there sometime,' and when Leo hesitated, Dominic resumed, 'I've heard you speak German, so the language won't be a problem.'

'I don't think you'd like it so much,' then, seeing Dominic's disappointed expression, Leo relented, 'we could think about it for later in the year. However, although I've spoken to Isabel McGuire and conveyed my condolences, I must phone her again, possibly tomorrow.'

'I know Ralph had Alzheimer's but do you know what happened?'

'I think he died from an overdose but I don't know the details. Sinclair said the police are still making enquiries.'

'Euthanasia?' hazarded Dominic. 'Obviously, Ralph's condition was deteriorating. Perhaps he couldn't face the final indignities?'

'And who could blame him?' said Leo.

Later that evening, Leo was drinking a Campari soda, deep in thought. Dominic's reference to his fluency in languages had brought back many memories, particularly the occasion when, while walking in St James's Park, he was addressed in German and had replied in the same language. The speaker had called him Manfred, enquired when he was returning to Vienna and looked puzzled when Leo insisted it was a case of mistaken identity.

The incident was forgotten until he received a phone call from Mervyn, an old school friend who worked at the Foreign Office, inviting him to lunch and enquiring if he was free that same afternoon. The conversation had switched from one language to another, covering various subjects. Leo recalled that he had been even more surprised when he was shown into a large office where two smartly-dressed, middle-aged men, who were introduced as Mr Smithers and Mr Price, simultaneously exclaimed, 'It's incredible!'

He had then learnt about the Waldner family, that Helmut, a wealthy businessman, was now involved in politics and that Manfred, who it was hoped would succeed his father, had succumbed to an extremely rare disease. Eminent physicians, diagnostics and specialists of different nationalities had examined Manfred and, while none were able to suggest or prescribe a definite cure, one had spoken of a drastic and prolonged treatment. This could take as long as three years and while his parents were anxious that Manfred should have this, they did not want his illness to become general knowledge.

Leo replenished his glass, recalling Smithers asking, 'Will you help us, please?' and Price elaborating, 'We would like you to go to Vienna, live with the Waldners and eventually impersonate Manfred.'

Price had then said that Leo would be expected to live in Vienna for three years, that a new and suitable wardrobe would be provided, travelling expenses covered, that he would be adequately recompensed and that he would be assured of good roles and a successful career on his return.

Between them the two men had pointed out that he was the same height and build as Manfred, his hair and eyes the same colour and that he spoke perfect German and French. Smithers emphasised that an early reply would be appreciated while Price suggested that Leo should tell family and friends that he would be spending the time in Europe.

It was as they reached the pavement that Mervyn said, 'You didn't mention the possibility of meeting and falling in love with an Austrian girl.'

Leo recalled that his reply had been brusque. 'That's highly unlikely, I'm not interested in girls,' and Mervyn has replied, 'Neither is Manfred.'

12

'I'm up to date with my reading. Would you like me to start packing up Ralph's clothes?' asked Elspeth, watching Isabel help herself to marmalade. They had discussed this the previous evening and agreed that everything should go to the Salvation Army.

'Yes, please. I did think of tackling it today, but not until this afternoon. There's a section of the current chapter I'd like to amend while it's still fresh in my mind.'

It was later that morning. Isabel had completed and was editing the current chapter while Duncan was drafting the next chapter, and both were startled when Elspeth suddenly appeared in the open doorway, exclaiming 'Guess what I've found!'

'Another will?' suggested Isabel while Duncan, noting the bulging envelope, hazarded, 'School reports?'

'No. These are all newspaper cuttings, years old. I

only glanced at the top one – they're all in chronological order.'

'Where did you find them? What are they about?' asked Isabel.

'Why are you so excited about them?' enquired Duncan.

'It was the photograph in the top cutting.' Elspeth extracted and passed part of a yellowing page to Isabel as Duncan stood up and peered over her shoulder.

'Good heavens; it's Leo as a young man!' exclaimed Isabel, gazing at the faded photograph.

'That's what I thought until I looked at this.'

Isabel took the remainder of the page and peered at the small print. Duncan did the same and it was he who said, 'That's Manfred Waldner, son of Helmut and Olga Waldner. Manfred died years ago, when he was only a young man, about twenty-five, I think. His father had a heart condition and it was hoped that Manfred, with his education and political potential, would carry on the family tradition.'

Taking the next page that Elspeth proffered, Duncan studied this, agreed that the top of the pages had been cut off and commented, 'There's no name to indicate which paper these came from, or any date.'

'You still haven't told us where you found this,' said Isabel.

'In the drawer where Ralph kept his underwear. It was under the lining paper and, before you ask, there's nothing in any of the other drawers.' Then, as Isabel reached for an album which she had brought back from Sidmouth, 'What are you looking for?'

'This.' Isabel deftly flicked through the pages and placed the faded photo next to a studio portrait of Leo when Elspeth and Duncan simultaneously exclaimed, 'It's incredible! What a remarkable resemblance.'

'You're the history expert. Can you enlighten us, please?' asked Isabel.

'It happened in the early seventies. The Waldner family were well known for several reasons: their wealth, town and country residences, Helmut's intellect and political powers, Olga's beauty and Manfred's inherited genius. Although Manfred's death was a terrible shock, his working and social life had remained unchanged, there had been no indication of any illness: it appeared that his parents and close relatives accepted this, almost as though it was expected.'

'What was the cause of his death?' asked Elspeth while Isabel, still gazing at Leo's photograph, said quietly, 'This coincides with the years we have nothing on Leo.'

Elspeth and Duncan exchanged amused glances and it was the former who said, 'You're not still thinking that Leo spent that time impersonating—'

'You must agree that they look alike,' interrupted Isabel and in the same breath, 'I must phone the inspector. He asked to be advised of anything unusual.'

Isabel began to dial, ignoring Elspeth's protest that this had happened years ago. It couldn't possibly have anything to do with Ralph's death.

'Where did you find them?' asked Detective Inspector Kershaw as he studied the faded photo and noted the attached cuttings. He then listened as Elspeth explained, and Duncan again related the tragic story of the Waldner family. During the short time that this took, his gaze travelled from the faded photo to that of Leo in the open album, and he now muttered, 'The resemblance is uncanny.'

'That's why I had this idea.' Isabel looked across at the inspector and continued. 'I agree with the others that it sounds ridiculous but suppose, as either could be mistaken for the other, and in view of Manfred's debilitating illness, that Leo was asked to impersonate him.'

'Is this relevant?' Kershaw's gaze travelled to Elspeth and Duncan but Isabel ignored this and persisted. 'The acceleration of Manfred's illness was at the same time as the three-year period for which we have absolutely nothing on Leo Adare.'

Kershaw shook his head, perplexed and turned to Elspeth again. 'Why did your brother hide these cuttings?'

'I've no idea. It all happened a long time ago, when he was a young man. Ralph wouldn't have noticed the resemblance; he didn't know Leo at the time. He hadn't been to Austria and didn't go in later years, so it's possible he was struck by this tragedy and thought of doing research on this family and writing about them. Even then he was interested in biographies. They were the only books he ever read, but why he kept these cuttings in that particular drawer, I don't know.'

At this, Kershaw turned to Isabel, but before he could speak the phone rang when, with an effort to remain composed, Isabel said, 'Good morning, Mr Adare,' then, in reply to his query, told him that with Duncan's help she hoped they would be able to meet Hugo's deadline. 'However, we do have a problem, there's a period of approximately three...'

Isabel rubbed her ear as Leo rang off abruptly and looked at Kershaw. 'There was no need for him to do that. It's not as though I asked him anything irrelevant.'

'But you were going to ask him about that gap?' hazarded Elspeth, aware that the inspector was watching her closely and when Isabel nodded, 'Perhaps Hugo would ask him?'

Kershaw indicated that he would wait, listened to the one-sided conversation and then Isabel told them, 'Hugo is as curious as we are. They're meeting for lunch next week when Leo returns from Venice. Apparently, when the biography was first discussed, Hugo asked if there was anything controversial which could come to light when Leo merely shrugged and said there was nothing untoward in his life.'

'You might have stirred up a hornets' nest,'

commented Duncan while Elspeth volunteered, 'It might be something really interesting that would help sell the book.'

Kershaw had followed the conversation with interest and now said, 'Will you let me know if Mr Forrester does learn anything of importance or relevance and, although I can't see that the discovery of these cuttings can have anything to do with your husband's death, can I borrow them?'

'We'd prefer not to part with the originals,' and picking up a bulky foolscap envelope, Isabel handed this to Kershaw. 'However, in spite of them being rather faded, Duncan has photocopied them.'

It was soon after he had spoken to Isabel that Leo realised he had ended the conversation rather abruptly and, by doing so, he might have made her even more suspicious. He then told himself that it had all happened a long time ago and, without going into great detail, he might be able to explain this period by saying that he had spent that period in Europe. He knew that Smithers and Price had retired, but it was possible that Mervyn might be able to advise him.

Ten minutes later, Leo replaced the receiver, reflecting

that Mervyn was a feeble and ineffective individual. He had muttered pleasantries but, in reply to Leo's request, had blustered and said he would have to refer to someone in a more senior position.

While Leo was criticising Mervyn's ineptitude, Mervyn was considering Leo's request. Although he was not a theatre-goer, he had followed Leo's career, noting that in spite of the favourable reviews Leo was not a household name, and had heard about the biography. He knew, having met him soon after his return, that Leo had slipped back into England very quietly, unperturbed that Manfred had died and that his parents were very distressed. Within a week, Leo had auditioned for a role in a drama soon to be produced in Chichester and from then on he had acted in different parts of the country and eventually, London. Little mention had been made in any of the reviews of his earlier years, his time at RADA and touring with repertory companies, and Mervyn doubted that anyone would really notice the three-year gap in the biography.

'What do you think about those?' Kershaw indicated the cuttings, 'and what about Isabel's ideas?'

'It must have been a terrible time for Manfred's parents. They had everything – position and wealth but their only son was very ill. I suppose you can understand them not wanting everyone to know about this, but someone must have seen Leo to know about the incredible likeness.' Tom paused. 'If Leo did stand in while Manfred was receiving treatment, which his parents no doubt hoped might cure him, he wasn't doing anything illegal. On the other hand, he didn't want those three years included in his biography; it might look as though he was bribed to play that role.'

'Which he was, really, and when he came back he fell on his feet, theatrically. Whoever arranged his stay in Vienna had connections with people in the theatre and it all worked out very satisfactorily. He's not another Richard Briers or Kenneth Brannagh but he's certainly done well financially: a flat in London, cottage in the Mendips, trips to the Far East or Caribbean, not to mention weekends in Venice, Rome or Monte Carlo.'

'He wasn't so generous when Zak Amory was living with him,' ventured Tom.

'That young man doesn't hide his dislike for Leo, but I can't see that he'd gain anything if the biography wasn't completed. And he wouldn't know about Vienna. The only person who might know, even though he was living in England, is…' Kershaw hesitated and then grinned as he and Tom exclaimed together, 'Baumgarten!'

And it was the latter who said, 'He didn't tell us about his life before coming to England.'

'There wouldn't have been anything untoward; he was only eleven years old at the time,' said Kershaw but nodded when Tom reminded him that Stefan still had elderly relatives living in Austria. 'But we don't know their name.'

'You're not going to suggest he could be related to the Waldner family?'

'Coincidences are happening all the time.' Tom glanced at his watch. 'Would Stefan have returned to the hotel yet?'

'Try his home number but I'll speak to him.'

Tom watched as Kershaw's expression changed to one of surprise. The conversation was brief and, as usual, Tom was curious; but this changed to astonishment when Kershaw said, 'Not only did he know the family, he was related. However, there's more to it than that. We're seeing him tomorrow morning when he'll tell us the whole story.'

13

'So you can understand, Inspector, why I was so upset.' Stefan Baumgarten had just recounted his relationship and friendship with Manfred, and their early years together in Vienna. This had been brief, but as he described his cousin's illness, his uncle's instructions that no one should know of this, and his suggestion that Leo Adare should stand in while Manfred received prolonged treatment, Stefan's voice was subdued.

'I know it was thirty years ago, but the thought of it still upsets me. I told Uncle Helmut that I didn't agree with his idea of withholding the news of Manfred's illness and, although I only met him on each holiday, I didn't like Adare.' Absorbed in his sad memories, Stefan did not notice Kershaw and Tom exchange glances. 'It made me sick to see him acting the affectionate son when in company – he looked and even sounded like Manfred. Leo certainly landed a plum role there.'

'How did your uncle hear about him?'

'A business associate saw Leo in London, thought

he was Manfred and spoke to him in German.' Stefan's voice was bitter. 'If his impersonation of Manfred became known, a publisher would probably want a detailed account of how those three years were spent which, although Aunt Olga and Uncle Helmut are dead, would still upset other distant relatives. Leo was out of the country as soon as Manfred died and his parting words to my aunt were heartless. Then, as you probably know, he landed on his feet, another plum role, and his future was assured.'

Stefan's gaze travelled from Kershaw to Tom and back again. 'I'm not happy about the biography, as you know, but if Ralph and Isabel hadn't agreed to do it, Leo would have found someone else.' Stefan paused. 'There's something else that surprised me, but it's nothing to do with Adare. As you know, Joanna is our head receptionist, and although it was only to be expected that she was upset about the circumstances surrounding her uncle's death, I was very surprised that she was so distressed about Isabel being so ill.'

'Interesting, but as I'm sure you're aware, we're still making enquiries as to how this happened,' said Kershaw and, standing up, thanked Stefan for his time and assistance.

'Well, what are you bursting to say?' asked Kershaw as they reached the car.

'Did you notice those white and yellow flowers?' and when there was no immediate reply, 'On that tree at the bottom of the garden, in the right hand corner?'

Kershaw nodded. 'Pretty, but why are you so excited?'

'That's a laburnum tree and, as you know…'

'The berries are poisonous and although we haven't heard from the toxicologist, could have been used to poison Isabel.' Then, with an expression of horror spreading over his face, Kershaw exclaimed, 'My God! That means one of the Baumgartens…' and stopping abruptly, 'no, it couldn't have been either of them. They had no occasion to go into the kitchen and wouldn't have known which plate was Isabel's.'

'The hedge between the gardens isn't very high, so the tree was within easy reach from Kieran's garden, and still on the subject of gardens…' Tom paused for breath while Kershaw silently admired and approved his young sergeant's enthusiasm, 'Did you notice how easy it would be to get into the Baumgartens' garden?'

As they fastened their seat belts, Tom continued, 'The hedge at the bottom of the garden was quite thin; anyone could get through quite easily. Suppose someone did that, got into their kitchen or through the French window in the lounge, and borrowed Stefan's hat and coat?'

'It couldn't have been Kieran; he was working,' Two waiters had confirmed that, as restaurant manager, Kieran had been on duty during the whole of the wedding reception. Kershaw resumed, 'It had to be someone who knew the Baumgartens were out for the day and also knew the couples who lived on either side were also out.'

'Marina knew and she was home on her own. She's tall, well built; the hat and scarf would cover her hair.'

'But why?' Then, aware of a sudden change of subject, Kershaw asked, 'Are you sure that was a laburnum tree?'

'Yes,' and when Tom told him that his grandmother had one in her garden Kershaw explained that, although he may have seen one on a previous occasion, he hadn't known what it was.

'This means that either Kieran or Marina, maybe both of them, realised there was a dangerous, could be lethal, poison at hand.' Kershaw had been amazed that, in spite of his excitement, Tom had driven across the Downs at a sedate speed and remained calm in spite of the flow of traffic and irate drivers at the top of Blackboy Hill. Kershaw reflected that there had been no point in turning back to call on Kieran as both he and Marina would be at work and now asked, 'Can you remember what Kieran said about dishing up and serving the food?'

Tom looked thoughtful. 'Kieran told us that as he dished up the boeuf bourgignon, he asked Marina to take the first two in for Belinda and Isa—'

'So, in a matter of seconds, Marina somehow sprinkled or mixed the berries in Isabel's food,' interrupted Kershaw.

'Which means she had it ready – it was premeditated. But why would Marina disguise herself to see Ralph McGuire, or want to poison Isabel?' Tom then answered his own question with, 'She knew Kieran didn't like his uncle or approve of the biography,' then seeing Kershaw's sceptical expression, Tom conceded that was hardly a motive. But after a momentary pause, 'She may have another reason; we don't really know a lot about her.'

'That's true,' agreed Kershaw, thinking they knew that Marina was a travel writer, still worked as a stand-by air courier and also for a travel company who provided escorts for visiting businessmen who wished to see some of the historical places in Bristol and the surrounding countryside. Marina and Kieran had been together for six years, but they had no knowledge of her background.

'What would she gain by Ralph's death and the attempt on Isabel?' Tom glanced sideways as he spoke, then his gaze was back on the road ahead. 'I suppose if Isabel had died, Elspeth would have inherited everything, which is quite considerable.'

'Are you suggesting that Ralph's death and the attempt on Isabel were for monetary gain?' And when Tom nodded, 'Apart from Joanna, there isn't anyone else who has a claim against Ralph's estate.'

'Not according to our knowledge.'

'What do you mean?'

'We don't really know much about Ralph's private

life before Isabel, and he wasn't young when he married her. You must agree that neither Isabel nor Elspeth were very forthcoming when we asked if they knew of anyone with a motive, or who would benefit from Ralph's death. It's still possible that, with prompting, Elspeth might be able to tell us something.'

'Isn't your…?' Kershaw stopped abruptly; he didn't want to dishearten his young sergeant who was so keen and instead he asked, 'Apart from questioning Elspeth again, how would you suggest we go about this?'

'There would be a record, either locally or at St Catherine's, if Ralph was married before and there were any children.'

'What are you implying, Sergeant'

On their return to the station, a phone call to Elspeth had resulted in an immediate visit to the McGuire household in Clifton; she now regarded the two detectives with annoyance and consternation. 'I can't imagine Ralph being interested in a young student, however attractive she was. He told me, in confidence, that he married Isabel because she was very intelligent and hard-working. He never said that he regarded her as attractive, which she was at the time, and I'm really pleased that she's taking more interest in her appearance.'

'There might have been occasions when, after a few drinks, your brother…'

Kershaw paused and Elspeth admitted, 'I suppose anything is possible. But why all these questions?'

Kershaw had delegated a DC to visit the local registry office but realised a trip to London might be necessary, and now said, 'We've spent too long making enquiries about Adare's biography and are now exploring other avenues. However, should you think of anything that happened when your brother was a young man, please let me know.'

'I'm sorry to bother you again, Mr O'Brien, but I'd be glad if you could spare us a few minutes. Is Miss Bushell in?' Inspector Kershaw had waited until half past five when he knew Marina was usually home.

'Please come in, Inspector and yes, Marina came in about two minutes ago.'

Kershaw immediately noted that Kieran was genuinely shocked on learning about the laburnum tree. 'I've noticed the flowers but I don't know anything about trees of any kind.' Kieran turned as Marina entered the room. 'Did you know that the tree in the corner of the Baumgartens' garden was a laburnum and that its berries are poisonous?'

'What berries?' Marina sounded vague, but Kershaw was not taken in by the indifference in her voice. However, it was Tom who volunteered, 'They're in the pods, which are about one and a half inches long; therefore, you wouldn't have seen them.'

'So what's all the fuss about?'

'The berries were the cause of Mrs McGuire being so ill.'

'That's ridiculous,' retorted Marina.

'I beg to differ.' For the last few days, Kershaw had been frustrated that he had not received any results from the toxicologist but, after Tom's discovery and on his return to the station that morning, he had taken immediate action.

The toxicologist had immediately apologised and interrupted Kershaw's explanation with, 'That's it. Laburnum! My assistant and I both came to the same conclusion earlier this morning. I was going to email you my report this afternoon.'

Bearing this in mind, Kershaw now said, 'I'm sure you must have seen the flowers and possibly the pods on the tree.' Marina shrugged but Kershaw persisted, 'The tree is easily accessible from your garden.'

'If you're suggesting that one of us reached across and took some of these pods I think you're forgetting something,' said Kieran. 'I've already told you I can't tell one tree from another.'

Kershaw nodded. His gaze had been on Marina and he now asked, 'Did you know that tree was a laburnum, that its berries were poisonous, Miss Bushell?'

'No. How would I know?'

Aware that Kieran was looking at his watch and becoming impatient, Kershaw told him, 'It's all right, Mr O'Brien, you can go. I appreciate that you're due back at the hotel.' Then turning to Marina, 'You could have read about them.'

'You can't leave me here being questioned by the police,' protested Marina as Kieran reached for his jacket.

'I'm sorry, I must go but I'm sure you'll be all right.'

Although he had never seen one before, Kershaw persisted. 'Are you sure you've never seen a laburnum tree before you came here, Miss Bushell?'

'No. Why should I want to poison Isabel McGuire?' Marina sounded belligerent as she continued, 'I'd never met her before.'

'She's lying. It must have been her,' said Kershaw five minutes later as Tom turned onto the main road.

'What do you propose to do, question their neighbours?' asked Tom and when Kershaw nodded, 'Perhaps her grandparents had one in their garden in which case the Bushells' neighbours would know and, although she denies it, Marina would recognise the flowers.'

My God! He's a clever young man, thought Kershaw and agreed that enquiries should be made.

By now, Kieran had reached Whiteladies Road but the inspector's questions were still uppermost in his mind. It was incomprehensible that Marina had poisoned Isabel, someone she didn't know but, in spite of her adamant denial, who else could have done it, and how? It had only taken a moment or two for her to carry the main course for Belinda and Isabel from the kitchen to the dining area of the lounge; however, Isabel had been poisoned. Fortunately, she had recovered, and it was obvious Kershaw was determined to find the person responsible.

Meanwhile, back at the hotel and knowing that the evening would be busy – a silver wedding anniversary in one private room and a retirement party in another – Kieran checked that everything was set out in readiness in the two function rooms to be used. As he drove to work, he had thought about the inspector's inference that laburnum berries had been used to poison Isabel McGuire, but now, still checking that the table linen, glasses, and cutlery were immaculate, Kieran dismissed all thoughts of Marina and the poisonous berries.

Duncan picked up the phone on the first ring and was startled when a muffled voice said, 'If you value your life, stop working on Adare's biography.'

'What are you talking about?'

'Isabel nearly died, Ralph did; it could be your turn next.'

'Who are you?' demanded Duncan, but it was too

late. The caller had rung off. Shrugging and thinking it was some silly fool trying to scare him, Duncan reached for his notes on the penultimate chapter and soon became engrossed in his work.

It was later that afternoon, and Duncan was standing, waiting for the traffic lights to change at a busy crossing, just beyond the Victoria Rooms, when he felt himself being pushed towards the edge of the pavement and the fast-moving traffic. Retaining his balance, he spun round to find a short, white-haired woman gazing up at him. 'Changed your mind, luv? You don't want to cross over?'

A plastic carrier in each hand, it would have been impossible for her to push him and, unaware that people were staring, he lowered his voice: 'Did you see where the person standing behind me went?'

'No. People were getting impatient, some moving away.' Then as the lights changed, she asked, 'Are you going, or staying here?'

'Going.' As they reached the opposite pavement, Duncan noticed she was looking rather tired and asked, 'Have you far to go? Can I carry your shopping?' And when she stared up at him in astonishment, 'I won't run off with it.'

'That's very kind of you. I only live round the corner,' and relinquishing the carriers, 'but they are rather heavy.' Turning off the main road, away from the noise of the traffic, she asked, 'Won't your friend be looking for you?'

For a moment, Duncan was at a loss, then remembering his original question he quickly fabricated, 'We didn't have a definite arrangement. He probably changed his mind.'

'There were several people in front of me, and being rather short, I couldn't see who was directly behind you.' And, in the next breath, 'Ah, here we are.' Stopping outside a tall grey-stone house, Duncan's companion gazed up at him again. 'I recognise you. You've been on television, haven't you?'

'No, but you may have seen my photograph on the cover of one of my books.'

'That's it, you're Duncan Sinclair! You write those lovely historical novels. I've read every one and thoroughly enjoyed them. And to think that you have carried my shopping home for me. By the way, my name is Eunice Cole. Can I offer you a cup of tea?'

'That's very kind, but no, thank you.'

Duncan waited until Eunice had unlocked the front door, then the door into what was obviously the ground floor flat, handed over her carriers and as he walked down the path could hear her saying, 'Well, fancy that! Meeting someone famous – my friends will be jealous.'

When Detective Inspector Kershaw had first met Marina, he had been interested to learn about her work as an air courier but now, late Friday afternoon, he groaned with frustration. This was not team work, so there had been no colleagues to question.

At the same time, Detective Sergeant Small had spoken to the personnel officer of the travel agents for whom Marina had worked. Although this had been six years ago, Tom learnt that Marina had been an excellent courier, always cheerful and courteous to the holiday-makers and capable of dealing with emergencies. She was also knowledgeable about the culture, customs, food and wines of the countries to be visited. Unfortunately, there were only two couriers who had known her still working for the company; they were on tour until Sunday evening and would both be available on Monday.

Marina's date of birth had been given by both companies and this had immediately been passed on to the constable at the registry office, but there had been no record of her birth having been registered there which meant that it would be necessary to check at St Catherine's.

However, by midday Saturday, Kershaw and Tom were amazed to learn that Marina was Ralph McGuire's daughter! She had been born in a London hospital and her mother, Felicity Bushell, had given Ralph's name as the father. 'Unless her mother told her when she was younger, she must have known that ever since she applied for her own passport,' said Tom.

'We know Ralph has not seen any visitors for the last two years; however, I wonder if she ever tried to see him before his condition deteriorated – she's been in Bristol for six years,' said Kershaw.

'And if her mother did tell her, Marina has known that he was her father for some time. It's possible that her mother, or even maternal grandparents, blackened Ralph's name to the extent that she didn't want to know him,' offered Tom.

Kershaw studied the photograph of Ralph McGuire on the back of his latest biography. It had obviously been taken several years ago, and he considered that McGuire had not been good-looking. A high forehead lengthened his already long and heavy face, bushy eyebrows drooped over deep-set eyes while a prominent nose emphasised thin lips. There was certainly no family resemblance between him and Elspeth, who was a very attractive woman.

'The news that Ralph had an illegitimate daughter will be a nasty shock for Isabel and Elspeth.'

Tom's voice broke into Kershaw's thoughts who, in spite of this, said, 'It's not for us to tell them.'

14

'Are you hurt? Would you like to lean on me?' Duncan was grateful for a shoulder to lean on and winced as he put his foot to the ground.

'Thanks, I'll be fine in a moment.'

Duncan glanced at the broad-shouldered young man who had grabbed and pulled him back from the constant stream of traffic that was coming up Whiteladies Road. Again, he had felt a hand pushing him forward and was surprised when his rescuer said, 'I saw an arm reaching out, the gloved fingers pressing against your back,' and, indicating a nearby tea shop, 'would you like a cup of tea? Or shall I accompany you home?'

'There's really no need,' said Duncan, then noting the concerned expression, relented, 'yes, let's have a cup of tea.'

Surprised at such courtesy from a complete stranger, Duncan was even more surprised when a waitress greeted his companion, 'Hullo, Sergeant, still hungry? What would your friend like?'

Tea and toasted teacakes ordered, Duncan looked at the young man sat opposite him and asked curiously, 'Are you in the habit of rescuing careless pedestrians?'

'That was deliberate. I'm just sorry that I didn't go after the person who pushed you.' After exchanging names, Duncan watched as Norman poured the tea and found himself recounting what had happened on Friday and the phone call.

'Sounds as though someone's got it in for you. Have you any enemies, or could they be jealous of your literary success?' Norman licked the butter off his fingers and grinned at Duncan's expression. 'I recognised your name. My mother's an avid reader and a great fan of yours. She's read all your books.' And before Duncan could reply, 'Have you had any more phone calls?' and still with apparent concern, 'I only just grabbed you in time. Do who know who the caller was?'

'No, the voice was muffled,' and in reply to Norman's next query, 'It must be someone who knows that I'm working with Isabel McGuire.'

'And followed you when you finished work.'

Although Norman said he only had a fleeting glimpse of someone pushing their way through the crowded pavement on the opposite side of the road, Duncan thought the young sergeant had probably noted some detail and volunteered, 'Eunice Cole said she was too short to see who pushed me on Friday.'

Norman knew that this had happened at a busy crossing near the Victoria Rooms and now learnt that

Duncan had accompanied Eunice home, and made a note of her address. Then, looking up, he enquired, 'How is Mrs McGuire coping?'

'Very well, considering everything that's happened, which you probably know, especially if you're on Inspector Kershaw's team.'

'Although her husband's condition was deteriorating, it must have been very distressing that he died under such suspicious circumstances.'

'Yes, the mysterious visitor has yet to be identified. However, I mustn't detain you.'

Duncan reached for his wallet but Norman forestalled him. 'Please, let me do this.' And as they reached the pavement, 'How's your ankle? Would you like a lift home?'

'No, thanks; it's feeling much better, but give me your mother's address and I'll send her a copy of my latest book.'

Ten minutes later, Norman replaced his mobile in his jacket pocket and fastened his seat belt. Chief Inspector Kershaw had been surprised and somewhat alarmed to learn about Duncan Sinclair and requested that Norman, although off-duty, should come in to give him a more detailed report of what had happened.

'What have you done to your leg?' asked Isabel as Duncan limped across the study and sat down.

'I slipped off the pavement on my way home yesterday afternoon, but it's nothing serious.'

It was some time later that morning. Isabel was in the kitchen making coffee, so Duncan answered the phone and was startled to hear the familiar but muffled voice again: 'You're still alive, pity! Why don't you pay attention to what I'm saying? If you don't stop working on that stupid biography you won't be so lucky next time.'

'Why are you doing this? Who are you?'

Duncan was still holding the receiver. The caller had rung off abruptly as before, when Isabel's voice startled him. 'I don't want to be inquisitive but what's happening? Who was that awful person?'

Seeing her pale face and that her hands were shaking, Duncan stood up quickly and took the tray from her. 'Come and sit down.'

'You can tell me to mind my own business,' said Isabel, sitting down, 'Are you being threatened?'

'Is that why you're limping?' This came from Elspeth who was standing in the doorway holding a mug of coffee.

Duncan groaned with exasperation. 'You've enough worries without bothering about me.'

'Nonsense,' retorted Elspeth and Isabel together and the latter continued, 'What's been happening?'

Elspeth moved further into the study and leant against Isabel's desk, sipping her coffee as Duncan recounted the incidents that had occurred on Friday and the previous evening, and his encounter with Norman, the young off-duty sergeant who, as far as he could see, wouldn't inform Inspector Kershaw.

'But the inspector should know!' exclaimed Isabel while Elspeth said, 'Whoever it is knows about everything that has happened – Ralph, Isabel, and certainly doesn't want the biography to be completed.'

'But why? What is this person going to gain if we don't complete? As we said before, Leo will find someone else to work on it,' and without pausing for breath, Isabel told Duncan, 'phone Kershaw.'

After complaining that he didn't want to waste the inspector's time, Duncan duly did as he was told, then, replacing the receiver, he said, 'The inspector will be here early this afternoon and also wants to see both of you.'

'Have you any idea who the caller is and why he's so adamant about Adare's biography?'

'No.' Duncan was grateful that Kershaw had listened without interruption and resumed, 'I'm not sure it's a man. The voice is muffled and, although I'm quite capable of defending myself, definitely menacing. Whoever it is is very determined.'

Kershaw had been annoyed that in rescuing Duncan the young sergeant was unable to chase the offender and he now asked, 'Did you notice anything particular about any of the pedestrians waiting to cross?'

'There was a young couple standing next to me, but I didn't turn round to see who was behind. I didn't think there would be another attempt to push me off the pavement, and I was certainly very grateful to your sergeant.'

Kershaw nodded, well aware that Norman was a keen, observant officer but, as Duncan now knew him, not the man to ensure Duncan arrived safely at the McGuire household every morning, or his flat every afternoon. As he stood up, it occurred to Kershaw that Duncan had not been present when he questioned Isabel and Elspeth about Ralph as a young man and he now asked, 'Can you remember any of Ralph's girlfriends? Did he ever have any serious relationships?'

'I'm sorry; I can't help you in that respect, Inspector. I've never heard of Ralph's friendship with a young woman. As you probably gathered from his colleagues who attended his funeral, he was an ascetic, scholarly type and they, like myself, were very surprised when he married Isabel. I'm sure they would agree with me that his increased success, since his marriage, was due to her ability and hard work.'

'Thank you, Mr Sinclair. You've been most helpful,'

and as he stood up, Kershaw asked, 'is it convenient for me to see Isabel and Elspeth?'

'Yes, they're in the lounge.'

As he drove back to the station some fifteen minutes later, Kershaw considered it was a pity that, once again, neither Isabel nor Elspeth had been able to help him regarding Ralph's younger days.

His thoughts then turned to Marina and the little he knew about her. He had learnt that she had been a good worker while employed by the travel company but always short of money and envious of other people's good fortune. This information had been supplied by the two young women who had known her and still worked for the same company. He now wondered about Marina's present financial position.

Marina walked across the Downs towards the sea wall, angry and frustrated. Although it was a sunny and warm afternoon, she thrust her hands deeper into the trousers of a drab grey tracksuit and muttered to herself. She had been surprised when Duncan Sinclair answered the phone and spent the remainder of the morning wondering how he had escaped the heavy traffic thundering up Whiteladies Road. She had again turned and pushed her way through the crowd about to cross the road and quickly mingled with office workers and shoppers heading towards Blackboy Hill.

Marina's thoughts went back to the dinner party, when she had been jealous that Duncan should be so attentive to Isabel, who was also younger than she had expected. Even now, she recalled her anger that while no mention was made of Ralph or the biography, Isabel appeared to enjoy herself. Marina took a bar of chocolate from her pocket, broke off four squares and thrust the remainder back, remembering her visit to Ralph McGuire.

She had been eleven years old when she learnt that he was her father and had been preparing to spend part of the summer holiday in France with a school friend. This information had come as a great surprise. Until then, she had always thought that her father was dead, which was what she had been told. There were no photographs, and neither her mother nor grandparents had ever spoken about him. This continued, and any questions she asked about him were ignored and there was no suggestion that she should meet him and she had often wondered why her mother had bothered to tell her his name. She was fifteen when she heard two teachers talking about a new book, a biography written by Ralph McGuire, and was immediately curious about this and the man who had written it. What kind of person could ignore his own daughter? There had never been any birthday or Christmas cards from him, and she had again wondered, as she had done on many occasions, if he knew of her existence.

Years later, after she had met and was living with Kieran, she thought it was a coincidence that Ralph, her father, should be writing the biography on Kieran's uncle, Leo Adare. She knew that Leo had neglected his sister and nephew at a time when they were in need of help and was not surprised that Kieran did not approve of the biography.

The telephone directory had provided Ralph's address and she had easily found the large house when exploring the Clifton area. On the day in question, she had brushed past Joanna, who she knew was Ralph's niece and head receptionist at the same hotel as Kieran, and hurried up the stairs. She could clearly remember her reaction and what had happened during her brief visit…

Ralph had been leaning against propped-up pillows, his face drawn and haggard – the photograph that appeared on the dust cover of his latest biography had obviously been taken some time ago. The eyes that gazed at her were dull, the thick eyebrows and nose more prominent. *My God! He's my father but looks older than my grandfather did,* thought Marina. The faded eyes peered at her curiously, the thin lips moved but there was no sound. A bony finger pointed at her when it suddenly occurred to her that he wanted to know who she was.

Her words, 'I'm Marina, your daughter' were forced, then in a rush, 'I'm twenty-seven and my mother was Felicity Bushell.' Marina watched, mesmerised, as with harsh grunts and vague gestures, Ralph indicated that she should remove the hat, scarf and coat. Discarding these garments so that they fell across the white bedspread, Marina stood for a moment, tall and slim in black t-shirt and trousers, still finding it difficult to believe that the man in bed was her father.

He opened his mouth, his thin lips almost invisible, but still no sound came forth and his features distorted with frustration as he pointed to the empty glass and bottle on his bedside table, and the door leading to the bathroom. Pouring some lemon barley into the glass, Marina then crossed the bedroom, pushed the door open, at the same time thinking, *how awful! He could go on like this, probably get worse, for weeks or longer.* She remained in the bathroom a moment longer and then flushed the toilet.

As Marina moved towards the bed, Ralph leant forward and held out his hands, but she ignored this and held the glass to his lips when he thirstily gulped down the contents. Marina watched as he leant back against the pillows and a few seconds later closed his eyes. Then she returned to the bathroom, rinsed, dried the glass and replaced it on the table. Donning her coat, scarf and hat, she glanced around the room and, on reaching the hall, told Joanna, who was standing at the bottom of the stairs, that Ralph did not want to be disturbed.

Marina's thoughts were still of Joanna as she stopped at the sea wall. As Ralph's niece, Joanna would be included in his will – her mother had died five years ago – but was there anyone else who would be included?

As on previous occasions, Marina realised that Isabel, now fully-recovered, would be the main beneficiary and was frustrated that the solicitor's notice had not yet appeared in the local paper. How much longer would she have to wait?

15

'Can you tell me why there's so much trouble for the people writing your biography?' Leo and Hugo had met, as arranged, at a Soho restaurant where they had eaten on previous occasions, ordered their meal and exchanged pleasantries over their aperitifs until Hugo could no longer restrain himself.

'What do you mean?' Leo's insouciant attitude infuriated Hugo even further.

While he realised that Leo was probably doing it deliberately, he snapped, 'You know damn well what I mean. Ralph died under suspicious circumstances, Isabel almost died from food poisoning and now Duncan is not only receiving threatening phone calls, he was almost killed last Friday.'

'What!'

Leo set his glass down with a thump and leant forward. 'How do you know about this?'

'Isabel phoned me yesterday after a visit from Chief Inspector Kershaw who is in charge of the investigation into Ralph's death. Apparently, one of his sergeants rescued Duncan just in time. He was pushed off a pavement, nearly ended up under a constant stream of traffic.' Hugo was pleased to see that Leo was now genuinely concerned and he persisted, 'What is there about your biography that this person doesn't want it published?' and when there was no reply, 'Do they know what happened during that three-year period which isn't covered, and about which Isabel and I are also curious?'

'It isn't anything to do with my theatrical career, but I suppose I'd better tell you.'

Leo drained his glass at the same time as the waiter told them their table was ready, so that it was a few minutes later, seated in a secluded corner, that Hugo prompted, 'Whatever happened was a long time ago; why all this secrecy?'

Leo ate another mouthful of smoked salmon and looked thoughtful, as though choosing his words with care, then told Hugo about the Waldner family and Manfred's illness. 'I returned to England as soon as he died and resumed my career.'

Hugo stared at Leo throughout, automatically eating asparagus tips and hollandaise sauce, and then exclaimed, 'It's incredible! To think that you actually lived in Vienna as someone else, for that length of time and no one knew the difference,' and only with a momentary pause while their plates were removed, 'how did they find you?'

After Leo had related being mistaken for Manfred, his meeting with Mervyn, then Smithers and Price, Hugo said, 'This could be another book. Your life there, the people you met – everything. Why haven't you mentioned this before?' Hugo curbed his impatience as the main course was served and nodded when Leo said he had been sworn to secrecy. 'But that was thirty years ago. There can't be any of the family left who'll object – you told me Manfred's parents are dead.'

'There was a cousin, the same age as Manfred, but I can't remember his name. His parents had moved to England and he returned to Vienna at least once a year during the time I was there. He's the same age as me, of course, probably still alive and might object to any reference to Manfred's illness.'

'To the extent that he's responsible for all that's happened to the McGuire family?' Hugo knew that Kieran lived in Bristol and had met him when he lunched at the hotel, and now asked, 'Do you have any relatives, or can you think of anyone who might object to your biography?'

'My nephew, Kieran, but I doubt that he'd be bothered.' Leo ate the last piece of steak on his plate. 'As you know, very little has been mentioned about my family, but that was my decision; it's my biography.'

You conceited bastard, thought Hugo and then heard Leo say, 'My two elderly aunts will probably be disappointed but that's too bad. However, returning to the reason for our meeting: has Duncan been frightened off completing, or are they going to finish by the deadline?'

Hugo ignored this question by asking one of his own: 'What do I tell them about those three missing years? As you know, it doesn't run smoothly. That chapter needs something else.'

Leo nodded, 'That's what Isabel said, and I must admit I was rather abrupt when she asked about that, and the three-year gap.

'I spoke to Mervyn before we flew to Venice; he is going to see someone higher up and will contact me. Nevertheless, I'm sure I could include a few paragraphs to the effect that I spent those years in Vienna studying the culture and improving my German.'

Hugo nodded. 'That sounds as though it would be acceptable. Let me know when you've heard from Mervyn.'

Neither wanted sweet or cheese and Leo was happy to talk about Venice as they drank their coffee until, although he knew about Leo's young Jamaican lover, Hugo asked, 'But you didn't go alone, did you?'

'No. Dominic enjoyed it as much as I did and is looking forward to our next trip, wherever that is.'

The two men parted company outside the restaurant whereupon Hugo strolled towards Leicester Square, deep in thought. He was concerned about the threats that Duncan was receiving and worried that the police had not yet found the person responsible for Ralph's death.

'Where are you going?' Stefan Baumgarten looked at the skirts and jackets on the bed. 'You'll find those rather warm at this time of the year.'

'You know I'm not going anywhere.' Belinda smiled as Stefan removed his jacket and reached into the wardrobe for a pair of casual trousers. 'I'm sure you have one or two suits that need cleaning.'

'Thank you, my dear. You're quite right.'

Stefan placed two dark business suits on the bed and then reached for his Austrian overcoat. 'Do you mind taking this as well? It's time it was cleaned.'

'I might as well make my journey worthwhile. Is there anything in the pockets?'

'I doubt it.' In spite of saying this, Stefan felt in both pockets and then suddenly said, 'What's this?'

Belinda glanced up from folding another skirt. 'It's only a tissue still folded. Probably never been used…'

'I realise that, but how did it get there? You know I never use them, neither do you; therefore, we never buy any.' Stefan laid the offending square object on the bed. 'It's one of those from a Kleenex travel pack, with a patterned edge.'

Belinda looked puzzled. 'I've seen the packets but as you've just said, never bought any. So how…?'

'That's not the only thing; there are some hairs on the collar and they're certainly not mine.' Stefan indicated several strands of dark brown hair and, gazing at Belinda's blonde curls, 'or yours.'

For a moment, neither spoke and then, hesitantly, Belinda ventured, 'Does this mean what I think it does?'

Stefan nodded, removed his fedora from the shelf in his wardrobe and indicated two further strands, the same colour.

'Someone got in and... who? How?' And as she realised that an outsider had been in the house, Belinda exclaimed, 'Oh my God! We've been burgled.'

'I don't think so. Nothing has been disturbed or taken. However, I am going to phone the inspector,' and as Belinda moved towards the pile of clothes for the cleaners, Stefan continued, 'leave them for now and come downstairs.'

'So you've only just discovered this?' said Kershaw some fifteen minutes later as, standing in the bedroom, he looked down at the coat and hat.

'Yes.' Stefan quickly explained the reason he had taken the garments from his wardrobe when he had noticed the offending hairs and, touching the grey hairs around his bald patch, 'As you can see, they're certainly not mine, or Belinda's. In any case, she would be completely lost in my coat.'

Kershaw nodded, aware that Tom, his young sergeant, kept glancing out of the window and fidgeting, eager to speak. However, he had several questions to ask so Tom would have to wait. Instead, he said, 'We'll have to take these garments for examination by forensics. I believe you also have a scarf?'

Stefan took this from the shelf and placed it on the bed, saying, 'Obviously, I haven't worn any of these garments for several weeks. As you will remember, we were away for the day on the Saturday that someone was seen wearing an Austrian-style coat. But how could anyone get in?'

'Oh stop it, Stefan!' exclaimed Belinda. 'You're making me nervous.'

Kershaw immediately noticed Stefan's anxious expression and said quickly, 'Could we have a cup of tea, please, Mrs Baumgarten? And perhaps you could find us a large carrier to put these garments in.'

'Of course, Inspector. I'm sorry; I should have offered you some tea when you arrived.'

Stefan waited until he could hear the clatter of cups and saucers from downstairs when he started again, 'How did…?'

'Someone could have climbed through the hedge which separates Kieran's and your garden,' interrupted Tom. 'It is rather thin in places.'

Then, in reply to Stefan's next question, Tom suggested, 'They could have got into the house through your kitchen, or the French window in the lounge. And they probably came back the same way to return the garments.'

'Who knew you were going to be away all day?' asked Kershaw.

'I remember telling the heads of departments, who know I'm always off on Saturday and Sunday, that we were driving down to Minehead to see some friends. One of them, I can't remember who, asked if we were staying overnight. I had suggested it but Belinda wasn't keen, just for one night and now… you've seen for yourself she's upset someone got into the house. There's two questions I'd like to ask before we go downstairs: do you think the person who "borrowed" these garments was responsible for Ralph's death, and do you have any suspicions as to who this is?'

'I'm hoping that the identification of these hairs will tell us that.'

'Will that take long?' But before Kershaw could answer, Stefan resumed, 'I think we should go down before Belinda gets more upset.' It was as he was about to leave the room that Stefan turned back and pointing to the tissue that was still on the bed, said, 'That was in the pocket, shall I throw it away?'

'No!' Transfixed and speechless, Stefan watched as Kershaw produced and quickly put on a pair of transparent gloves, and gently ran his forefinger over the tissue. 'This has been used but for an unusual purpose. Something has been crushed in this.' Kershaw refolded the tissue then slid it into a small plastic envelope which he had taken from his jacket pocket. 'Thank you very much, Mr Baumgarten, for what might prove to be significant evidence. However, we won't mention this to your wife.'

Teacups and a plate of assorted biscuits were on a long, highly polished coffee table and Belinda, who had been looking out at the garden, still agitated, turned, indicated comfortable easy chairs and picked up the teapot. Kershaw, interested to learn about Stefan's life as a hotelier and his rise to his present position, was glad to see Tom was unobtrusively learning more about the day they spent in Minehead, their friends and also Marina. He was then surprised to hear Belinda ask, 'Has Isabel McGuire fully recovered? Will they be able to finish the biography in time?'

'Yes. I understand that Duncan Sinclair is a great help.'

'And very charming.' Stefan paused as he drank his tea and then resumed, 'Although I've never met her and her name wasn't mentioned at the dinner party, I gather Elspeth McGuire is a very attractive and intelligent woman.'

Kershaw nodded. 'Apparently, she and Isabel have been friends since their schooldays; they attended Redmaids,' and rising to his feet, 'we must be on our way.'

As he drove, Tom briefly recounted what he had learnt about Marina. Although neighbours for some time,

Belinda, who worked part-time in a charity shop, did not see Marina very often. She occasionally asked the younger woman over for coffee and, on each occasion, noted that Marina was constantly gazing around and then talking disparagingly about their own home and furnishings and her ambition to redecorate and refurbish this. 'That's the way she behaved when she was working as a full-time courier,' concluded Tom.

'We haven't heard anything from Peter Hoskins, so he obviously hasn't seen Marina,' said Kershaw. 'There hasn't been a legal notice in the paper yet which means she wouldn't know who to contact.' Kershaw had allocated this task to a keen young constable and resumed, 'I'll phone Hoskins when we reach the station while you organise a house-to-house team. Although the person wearing that hat, scarf and coat was only seen by Alex Gresham, it's possible they were also seen by someone living in the Henleaze area.'

'Very good, sir.'

'Why would anyone want to borrow your hat and coat and who, or rather how many people, know you own them?' Ten minutes had elapsed since Inspector Kershaw and his sergeant had left and, still sitting in the same armchair, Belinda gazed at Stefan who stood by the French window.

'I'm sure that's exactly what the inspector and his

sergeant are asking themselves.' Stefan had already phoned the locksmith and a man was already on his way to change locks and supply additional security fittings.

'I can't or rather I don't want to believe that the person who broke into our house was responsible for Ralph McGuire's death, can you?' asked Belinda.

'It's not for us to think or worry about that, my dear. Inspector Kershaw is in charge of the case and I'm sure he's more than capable of finding out what happened.'

'But if that person was wearing your hat and coat, would you be... what d'you call it, an accessory?'

'Of course not. There may be no connection whatsoever and you're worrying unnecessarily.'

'I can't help it.'

At that moment, the doorbell rang. Belinda became startled and Stefan calmed her by saying, 'That's probably the locksmith. I'm sure he would like a cup of tea.'

An hour later, after making the necessary adjustments and additions to the French window, kitchen, front doors and all ground floor windows, the fitter returned to the kitchen and his usual timid smile widened into a grin. 'I don't know what you're cooking, madam, but it smells wonderful. Unfortunately, my wife hasn't any imagination when it comes to food.'

Belinda smiled and relaxed. 'I suddenly remembered: I have a friend from the charity shop coming to supper. It's not a difficult dish and the ingredients aren't expensive. Perhaps your wife would like to try it if I gave you a copy of the recipe.'

Stefan, who was standing in the doorway, gave a sigh of relief. Belinda always enjoyed cooking or talking about food, and he was glad that she wouldn't be alone that evening. She usually invited one of the other helpers for a meal on Wednesday, which was one of his evenings on duty at the hotel. He now watched as Belinda jotted down the ingredients for a goulash and wished he could be home to enjoy it.

The young fitter was still sniffing appreciatively when he accepted the cooking instructions and quickly read them. 'Thank you very much, madam.' And as he reached the front door, Belinda heard him say, 'You're a lucky man, sir, to have a wife who can cook like that. There aren't so many women who can be bothered to prepare a proper meal; it's all microwaves and takeaways. They could learn a lot from your good lady.'

16

'This is all most interesting, Inspector. You're certain neither Elspeth nor Isabel know about this young woman?'

It was early Thursday morning and Kershaw, who had been very grateful when Peter Hoskins agreed to see him before his first appointment, had just recounted all that was known about Marina Bushell. 'Elspeth can't recall Ralph ever showing any interest in girls.'

Peter nodded. 'My first impression of him, which was when his parents died, was that he was definitely the academic type. Ralph wasn't good-looking, but tall and broad-shouldered. I realise that was years ago, but it was difficult to believe he was the same person. When I called at the house, about nine months ago, he had shrunk and was considerably thinner. Although it was sad that he should die so unexpectedly, in a way it was a happy release. He didn't have to suffer the indignities that so many with Alzheimer's endure.'

Peter looked at Kershaw and with surprising candour asked, 'I know you're still investigating the circumstances surrounding his death. Have you any idea who the mysterious caller was?'

'We're waiting for some results from forensics,' and without pausing, Kershaw asked, 'who would inherit if anything happened to Isabel?'

'Unless she willed it otherwise, Elspeth. As you already know, she's Ralph's sister, and Joanna was also included in his will. But returning to Isabel, do you know who was responsible for poisoning her? What was used?'

Peter's expression became grim as he learnt of the laburnum tree in the Baumgartens' garden, Kieran's lack of knowledge of trees and that enquiries were still being made. 'I realise it's a week since Tom recognised the tree as a laburnum, but the couple who live next door to the Baumgartens have been away. They're expected back this evening. One of the local officers will be calling on them tomorrow morning,' said Kershaw.

'So that was the reason for the question you asked just now. I'd be glad if you could let me know as soon as you hear anything.' Peter paused and then added, 'A notice regarding claimants against Ralph's will appears in the paper tomorrow, so I'm sure I'll hear from Marina.'

Meanwhile, Detective Sergeant Tom Small, together with Detective Sergeant Rowena Lovell, were both questioning Marina about her walk on the Downs on the Saturday afternoon that Ralph died.

Although Marina stated that she had been alone and seen no one she knew, Tom persisted, 'Surely on a Saturday afternoon there are regular walkers, people exercising their dogs? As a person who frequently walks there, it's surprising you didn't see someone you knew. Can you remember what time you left home and returned?'

It was at this juncture that Rowena said, 'Can I use your bathroom please, Miss Bushell?'

'Of course. It's upstairs, second door on the right.' Marina transferred her attention to Tom. 'I can't tell you exactly what time I left here and returned. Probably about half past two, and I suppose I got back about half past four, maybe a bit later.'

'We're very fortunate to have such a large area for walking, but before we continue, can I trouble you for a glass of water?'

Marina looked apologetic. 'I'm sorry, I should have offered you both some coffee.'

'There's no need for that, just some water please. I must have eaten something salty. I seem to have developed a raging thirst,' and in reply to Marina's query, Tom said that some ice would be most acceptable.

On his previous visit, Tom had noticed a photograph of Marina in her courier uniform and as soon as he heard her moving around in the kitchen, he quickly pulled a digital camera from his pocket and took a copy of this. He had just checked that this was satisfactory when he heard the clink of ice against the glass and was studying the contents of a crammed bookshelf when Marina reappeared and, as though there had been no interruption, he asked, 'Were you walking all the time? Did you sit down for a while? What were you wearing?'

'Good heavens, what is this – an inquisition? I was wearing my tracksuit and walking all the time.'

Tom nodded, wrote in his notebook but was not really satisfied with this answer, then Rowena returned and after a few remarks about Marina's work they thanked her for her assistance and left.

It wasn't until they reached the top of Blackboy Hill that Tom glanced at Rowena. 'Did you have any luck?'

'Yes, there was a scruffy grey tracksuit in her wardrobe and hairs in her brush and comb.' Rowena's eyes lit up as she continued. 'I also found an open packet of tissues. They look exactly the same as that Mr Baumgarten found in his coat. How did you get on?'

'Fine. Let's hope we've got a match with the hairs and tissue, and also the fibres from the coat that were found in Ralph's bed.'

'And that the old lady and Norman recognise Marina as the person at the traffic light.' Rowena, who was fair-haired and very slim, frowned. 'Marina's taller and generally bigger than me, but there's nothing outstanding about her.'

'If she intended to push Duncan off the pavement

she certainly wouldn't have been wearing anything in bright colours,' said Tom.

At the same time that Tom was advising Inspector Kershaw of Marina's reaction to his questions, Stefan Baumgarten was regarding Kieran with concern. They had just concluded a meeting with other heads of departments about forthcoming functions, the others had left and Stefan thought Kieran looked tired and dejected and asked, 'Are you feeling all right?'

'Yes. I'm fine, thank you. I'm pleased we're so busy.'

'Is anything worrying you? Do you want to talk about it?'

'Er… no, thank you.' Then in a rush Kieran said, 'I still can't make out how Isabel McGuire was poisoned. As I told the inspector, I'm always very careful when shopping.'

Stefan nodded. 'It's certainly strange, and although I hate asking this but I'm sure Kershaw did, could Marina have put anything in the boeuf bourgignon?'

'I suppose it's possible, but when? If she did, everyone would be affected.'

'That's true. So whatever was used was added when she brought in the main course for Belinda and Isabel from the kitchen.' Stefan gazed at Kieran. 'I've thought about this on a number of occasions, that it could have been Belinda who was poisoned. Damn it, the dinner party was over a fortnight ago. What are the police doing about it?'

'I don't know. We've both been questioned again and asked not to leave town without telling them. I told the inspector that I haven't any knowledge of poisons or the effect they would have which means…' Kieran shook his head and once again wondered how, despite her claim that she had no knowledge of laburnum trees, Marina had obtained and added the toxic substance. And why? She'd never met Isabel before – why did she want to harm her, possibly kill her? It was after the inspector's last visit that Kieran realised how little he really knew about Marina. She occasionally spoke about her mother, often mentioned her grandparents with whom she and her mother had lived until they moved into a residential home, but had never referred to her father.

'I'm sure the inspector has asked himself those questions over and over again.' Then, after a slight pause, Stefan asked, 'Has Marina been behaving differently lately? Talked about personal problems or anything to do with work?'

'No.' Kieran looked thoughtful. 'But she has been acting and talking very strangely. She's dissatisfied with the house, contents, everything.'

'When are you taking your holiday? Why don't you go somewhere completely different?'

'I'm taking a fortnight next month; but in spite of package holidays that are on offer, I do have a large mortgage.'

For a brief moment Stefan thought of Leo Adare, his Jamaican lover and lifestyle but, knowing Kieran's attitude towards his uncle, refrained from mentioning his name. Instead, he said, 'Perhaps Marina will hear of something.'

Kieran shrugged. 'I doubt that anything, however exotic, would satisfy her at the moment. She seems to be looking for a lifestyle that's far beyond our joint income.' Then pulling himself together, Kieran continued: 'I'm sorry about all that, Mr Baumgarten, but thank you for listening.'

'Any time, Kieran. I don't like to see you so depressed.' Then, as an afterthought, 'Although we've known Marina since you moved in, I've never heard her talk about her family. Are her parents still alive? Does she have any other relatives?'

'Her mother died just before her twentieth birthday and except for her maternal grandparents, she's never spoken about anyone else. However, I must get on. Once again, thank you for listening to me.'

Alone, and although there were various aspects of the hotel that required his attention, Stefan's thoughts were still of Marina. When he first met her, soon after she and Kieran had moved in – they had been in their respective gardens – she had seemed a pleasant young woman; but recently, just before the dinner party, Belinda had also remarked that Marina seemed sullen and dissatisfied. Stefan then considered the dark hairs on his coat. *Were they Marina's? Why should she break in and borrow his coat?*

The arrival of the advertising and marketing manager claimed Stefan's attention, and all thoughts of Marina were instantly dismissed.

'Did Mr Hoskins sound rather strange when he spoke to you this morning?' asked Elspeth as, placing a plate of assorted sandwiches on the kitchen table, she looked across at Isabel.

'No, but I must say I'll be pleased when everything is settled.'

Elspeth, who had answered the phone, therefore speaking to the solicitor first, nodded. 'The insertion of the claims notice is usual procedure, but in Ralph's case there shouldn't be any problems. You've dealt with all the finances for the last two years.'

'And there are no distant relatives who might think they're entitled to some of Ralph's money?' asked Isabel.

Duncan heard this as he appeared in the doorway and looking from one to the other, queried, 'Problems?'

'No, just the usual formalities,' said Elspeth, explaining that the legal notice regarding claims or debts against Ralph's estate would appear in the paper the next day.

'Knowing how efficient you both are, I can't foresee

any difficulties.' Duncan refrained from saying that since his conversation with the inspector on Tuesday, a nondescript young man had been following him to and from his flat, and continued, 'Those sandwiches look good.'

'Help yourself,' said Elspeth.

'I wonder when Hugo will hear from Leo,' mused Isabel. Hugo had advised her of his conversation with Leo and that he was awaiting definite instructions from the actor, but now she was eager to clarify the omission.

They were still sitting in the kitchen discussing the possible sale of the house when the phone rang. Duncan stood up, hoping it wasn't another threatening phone call, but Isabel was already answering the extension in the hall and her voice rose slightly as she said, 'Hullo, Hugo.'

Taking advantage of Isabel's absence, Elspeth said, 'I trust there's no problems on your walks from and back to your flat?'

'No.' Again, Duncan did not mention the young man and agreed when Elspeth said it was a pity the police were taking such a long time to find the mysterious caller. For the umpteenth time, Duncan wondered if this caller was the same person who had attempted to poison Isabel and push him off the pavement and briefly considered that if it wasn't Kieran then it must be someone who had been in his kitchen prior to the dinner party.

Isabel's voice broke into his thoughts. 'Leo has told Hugo we can minimise those three years, as he suggested.'

'What else did he say?' enquired Elspeth, noticing the sparkle in Isabel's eyes.

She knew that Hugo, only two years older than Isabel and a widower, was very fond of her, but this was quickly dismissed as Isabel said, 'Lady Fairburn has asked Hugo if I would consider writing her biography. She would like us to start as soon as that on Leo is completed.'

'She can't jump the queue just like that,' protested Duncan. 'You've had several other enquiries.'

'But only that – nothing has been agreed. And Lady Fairburn would like us to work as a team.'

'That'd be great, and most interesting. I've heard she's a charming and gracious old lady.' Elspeth watched as Duncan's expression changed. His smile lit up his handsome features while his body relaxed. For a moment, Elspeth recalled the years she and Isabel had spent at university, the same one as Duncan, and the fact that they had all been good friends. No, it had been more than that between Isabel and Duncan, thought Elspeth. She had been waiting for Isabel to confide in her then something had happened and Duncan had left unexpectedly. They later learnt that his mother had died, leaving him with the responsibility of a younger and physically handicapped sister. For a brief moment, she considered it strange that Duncan had not mentioned his sister since his return and wondered if she had also died.

Elspeth then heard Isabel say, 'Don't get too excited.

I've told Hugo we're not starting anything new until we've moved,' and looking at Elspeth, 'you're still quite happy about it?'

'Oh, yes! I really like the idea of somewhere smaller, without all this cumbersome old-fashioned furniture.

'Ralph was a real curmudgeon when it came to changes. I was always surprised that you were prepared to live here, in the old family house, when you married.'

'That's a long time ago.' Isabel's gaze travelled to Duncan. 'I'm sure we won't be all that far away.'

'I do have a car. It's just that I prefer to walk when I can and, by using a roundabout route, I can avoid the busy main roads.'

'I've spent most of my life in this house and, in spite of everything that's involved, I'm really looking forward to moving,' said Elspeth. 'I could have moved, found myself a flat, but somehow I was too lazy.'

'I wouldn't say that,' protested Isabel. 'You've always looked after Ralph, even after we were married. I'm amazed at your tolerance. I don't know how I could have got through the last two years without you, or even when Ralph was well. However, if you're not too busy this afternoon I do have a favour to ask.'

'What is it?'

Duncan noticed Elspeth sounded apprehensive, but her eyes lit up with excitement as Isabel said, 'Call in at some of the estate agents in this area. See what they have on their books.'

'How lovely! I shall enjoy myself.'

Delighted to see two smiling faces, Duncan spontaneously suggested, 'And I'll take you both out to dinner tonight.'

17

After a hectic lunch hour and with the prospect of a busy evening, Kieran was glad to return to an empty house. Marina was spending the day with a party of French teachers who were keen to visit and walk across the suspension bridge, and also visit the SS Great Britain and the Matthew.

It was a warm, sunny afternoon, so after changing into shorts and t-shirt, Kieran stretched out on one of the sunbeds on the patio, but in spite of the soothing music of his favourite CD he couldn't relax, unable to forget Stefan's enquiry about Marina's parents and other relatives.

A few minutes later, he was staring at Marina's birth certificate, aghast. It seemed impossible; how could Ralph McGuire be her father? But his name was written on the document, above that of Felicity Bushell, her mother. There were also letters from Ralph. Kieran hated himself for snooping in the drawer where Marina kept her passport, references, bank statements and other private papers and, as he replaced the certificate back in the envelope, he wondered how she could have deceived him for such a long time.

Had she ever visited Ralph, made herself known before he became ill, wondered Kieran. But he quickly dismissed this idea – Isabel had greeted her as a complete stranger. What did Marina intend to do now that Ralph was dead, Kieran asked himself. Did she intend to make herself known to Isabel at a later date, which would be a great shock and, in that instant, the idea occurred to him; was she going to contest Ralph's will? Marina had been in such a strange mood lately, very dissatisfied, that anything was possible. But what could he do? He certainly couldn't mention her birth certificate; she'd go berserk at the idea that he'd even opened the drawer.

By now, Kieran was pacing to and fro on the patio then decided that by talking about his uncle he could tactfully enquire about any distant relatives she might have. There had certainly been various occasions when he had spoken of his uncle that she could have told him that Ralph was her father, but she hadn't. However, worrying about this wouldn't do any good, so picking up a copy of John Francome's latest book, he made himself comfortable and, as usual, soon became engrossed.

To his surprise, Marina returned in good spirits; the courier who had been booked to accompany the French party to Bath the next day, and to Wells and Glastonbury on Saturday, had broken her ankle and she had been asked to take over these excursions.

Returning to the hotel, Kieran was surprised to learn that Duncan Sinclair had booked a table for three for dinner. 'He's bringing Isabel and Aunt Elspeth,' said Joanna and seeing Kieran's puzzled expression, 'she's Ralph's sister and they've always lived in the same house.' Marina knew about Joanna as Kieran had spoken about her on various occasions, but he now considered that Marina would be surprised to discover that she also had an aunt; then, after checking the list of other dinner guests, he returned to the dining room.

Marina let herself into the house and bent to pick up the *Evening Post*. It had only just arrived. The delivery boy had disappeared round the corner as she inserted the key. It was only half past four which meant that she had time to read the paper before Kieran, who always played squash on a Friday afternoon, returned. The excursion to Bath had been a great success, but they had all wanted to return early. There was a cocktail party followed by dinner when they would meet local business people and civic dignitaries.

Ten minutes later, Marina sat up with a jerk, staring at the paper – there, in print, was the notice asking anyone with claims against or debts owed by Ralph McGuire, to contact Hoskins and Rankin. Within seconds, Marina was talking to Peter Hoskins, trying to keep her voice even as she told him, 'I must see you. I'm Marina Bushell, Ralph McGuire's daughter. Unfortunately, he didn't marry my mother.'

'Do you have proof of that statement, Miss Bushell?' Hoskins had switched on his tape recorder as soon as he was advised of her call and nodded to himself as Marina told him that she had a birth certificate and letters from Ralph to her mother, and concluded, 'When can I see you?'

'We don't come into the office on Saturdays so it will have to be Monday.' Hoskins' diary was already open but he deliberately paused, 'And then I can just fit you in at half past nine. Please bring whatever documents you have with you.'

'Damn and blast!' muttered Marina. 'Now I've got to get through the weekend. Stupid old man! Why didn't he ask me to come in now, or offer to come in tomorrow?'

As arranged, Hoskins immediately informed Inspector Kershaw of Marina's call and said that he would be seeing her Monday morning. 'She wasn't very happy about that. I think she expected to come in now, or tomorrow.'

'That sounds rather typical of her. I'm sure she

won't be very happy until she sees you but don't let that spoil your weekend.' Kershaw was about to replace the receiver when he suddenly asked, 'Have you spoken to Isabel or Elspeth about this?'

'No. I don't think there's any point in doing that until I've met Marina. However, have you anything to add to yesterday's conversation?'

'Yes. A local sergeant called on the Bushells' neighbours who were both very voluble and happy to talk about Marina. Apparently, Frank Bushell was very knowledgeable about everything that grew in his garden. The neighbour had been a keen gardener himself and they would often see Marina and her grandfather walking around when he would ask her to identify the various flowers, shrubs and different trees. They both knew that Frank was very proud of Marina, her fluency in languages, but in particular, her interest and knowledge about everything that grew in his garden. Apparently, there was a laburnum tree in the Bushells' garden so Marina's adamant denial that she didn't recognise the tree in the Baumgartens' garden was another lie. As we already know, Stefan's neighbours saw her reach over the hedge and take something from the tree on the Saturday morning before the dinner party.'

'What do you propose to do now? Are you going to bring her in for further questioning?' asked Peter.

'No. We're still waiting for results from forensics.'

Kieran had noticed that Marina had been in an irascible mood ever since Friday and having seen for himself the legal notice regarding Ralph McGuire's estate, wondered if Mr Hoskins' reaction had upset her.

Knowing that she liked to talk about her trips with the different European businessmen who frequently visited Bristol, he learnt that the trip to Wells with the French party had been a great success. They had all been very impressed with the cathedral, reluctant to leave the lovely old building, and the quaintness of the city.

It was Sunday afternoon. They were sat on the patio browsing through the papers and he wondered if he should tell her that he had seen Duncan and Isabel on Friday evening, when he had been introduced to Elspeth McGuire. He had only met Ralph McGuire on one occasion, when he had lunched at the hotel, and again Kieran considered that Elspeth did not resemble her brother: she was an attractive and smartly dressed woman.

Kieran's thoughts about Elspeth were suddenly interrupted as Marina said, 'There's something I have to tell you. I should have done so a long time ago.'

Kieran dropped his paper, guessing what was coming, but in a light-hearted manner he joked, 'You've heard from one of your ex-husbands?'

'No, it's nothing like that. It… it goes back further.' Marina sat up straight and swung her feet to the ground so that she was facing him. 'I'm illegitimate. Ralph McGuire was my father.'

'Good God!' Kieran feigned surprise. 'Who told you that? His solicitor?'

'No. I've known for some time. My mother told me on my eleventh birthday. She had always told me my father died when I was a baby but felt it was time I knew the truth.'

'Did you get in touch with him, see him?'

'No, why should I after the way he ignored us? Apparently, my mother told him she was pregnant and later of my birth but, while he acknowledged this, he never asked to see me or offered any financial assistance.'

'The cold-hearted bastard!' exclaimed Kieran. 'Surely your mother could have…'

'No. She didn't want to get involved with anything like suing him for maintenance. Fortunately, my grandparents were very supportive.'

'Why didn't you tell me before?' And when there was no immediate reply, 'Have you seen him since you came to Bristol?'

'What do you think?'

Kieran had also moved so that he sat facing Marina. 'Then why are you telling me all this now?'

'Because I'm going to see Ralph's solicitor in the morning. Ralph ignored me during his lifetime. He could have made my mother's life easier, so why shouldn't I have something?'

Kieran was about to mention the dinner party when she had met Isabel but said, 'You'll need proof.'

'I've my birth certificate – Ralph's named as my

father – and letters from him to my mother. I intend to fight for whatever is due to me.' Marina gave a deep sigh and stood up. 'After all that I'm going to make some tea.'

Kieran leant back on his lounger, thinking he had contributed very little to the conversation and that Marina might not find it quite so easy to acquire what she considered her entitlement.

'I don't understand why, having lived in Bristol for the last six years, you didn't visit your father.' Peter Hoskins regarded Marina as he continued. 'Even though you were employed as a courier, which involved a lot of travelling, you still had many opportunities to do so.'

'I thought about it… I was apprehensive. It was a difficult situation and then I heard that he had become ill.'

'So you couldn't face up to his illness?' Peter had studied Marina's birth certificate and learnt that she had been told of her father's identity when she was eleven. He had questioned her about her mother and maternal grandparents and heard that they had never referred to or spoken about her father. He had scrutinised the letters from Ralph, particularly that one in which he acknowledged that Marina could possibly be his child, but there was no suggestion from him that he would have a blood test or would make an allowance towards her maintenance and later, her education.

He, Peter, also knew that Marina and her mother had lived in her grandparents' home until the time came when they admitted they couldn't cope with such a large house and garden. Mr and Mrs Bushell had moved into a residential home, one of the more luxurious kind. The house had been sold to pay for this and help towards the rent of the flat which her mother had taken.

'I was sorry that I didn't go when he was in good health.'

'So you've never been to the house? You don't know where…' Peter stopped abruptly. It wasn't for him to question Marina along these lines. In fact, he didn't like his predicament – that he was acting as a stool pigeon for the police. On the other hand, it was his duty to protect Isabel and Elspeth's interests and, aware that there was only three minutes before his next appointment, he said, 'I suppose you realise this, or rather your existence, will be a great shock to Isabel and Elspeth.'

'Who's Elspeth?'

'Ralph's sister, your aunt.' Peter noticed Marina's expression change and persisted, 'That is if you're really who you say you are.'

'Of course I am! You've seen my birth certificate, the letters and also my passport, but I need that for my work.'

Peter bit back the words… you could've picked

them up, stolen someone's handbag... thinking that was exactly what Kershaw would say and told her, 'There are certain formalities to be completed when something like this occurs. I'm sure you realise this could be a costly procedure.'

'But not if I get what I'm entitled to. That house alone must be worth a fortune...'

It was said before Marina realised, but Peter immediately recognised the mercenary streak, that Marina was an accomplished liar and said quietly, 'As you're aware, I'm acting on Ralph's instructions, so if you're claiming against the estate I can't act on your behalf.'

Marina pointed to the papers on the desk. 'You've the proof. Can't it be satisfied without all this legal fuss and bother? Couldn't I have a cheque for £5,000 – just to start with?'

'Of course not!' Peter was disgusted at this suggestion and his voice was brusque. 'I thought you were an intelligent young woman but now I doubt it. These things take time. It could be months, in some cases even years, before monies can be paid out of a deceased person's estate.'

'Surely you could hurry up the process?' persisted Marina.

'Probate hasn't been granted. It could take several months. Another thing: Isabel and Elspeth must be informed of your visit.' Peter stood up as he spoke. 'My next appointment is waiting for me. I'll be in touch.'

18

'Stupid old fool! He could easily have given me a cheque,' expostulated Marina as she stood on the pavement, unaware she was receiving curious glances from passers-by. Marina stood for a moment, staring into a window but not seeing the contents, then, glancing at her watch, realised she only had twenty minutes before she was to meet a party of German businessmen.

As she made her way to the hotel where the Germans and the minibus driver would be waiting for her, Marina's thoughts were confused. The knowledge that Isabel had completely recovered and Duncan had not suffered any injuries as a result of being pushed off the pavement was bad enough, but to learn that Ralph had a sister had certainly been a shock. And as for the solicitor – he had been very observant; she would have to be careful what she said when she next saw him.

For a moment, Marina remembered her grandparents' house – the high-ceilinged rooms, all spacious and tastefully furnished, large lawns and well-tended flowerbeds – which she had hoped would be hers. She had always thought they were very wealthy and had been bitterly disappointed when the house was sold.

Her thoughts then turned to the large house in Clifton. It was definitely too large for two women, and the furniture she had seen, and probably that in the other rooms, was dark and old-fashioned. If the house was modernised, redecorated and completely refurnished, it could look so different and she would really enjoy living and entertaining there.

Marina's expression was grim as she resolved that Hoskins would soon learn of her intention to have the larger part of Ralph's estate.

'There's something about that young woman I don't like,' said Peter Hoskins. 'For a start she's a liar, and she's greedy – she wanted something at once, £5,000 – would you believe it? And is she really Ralph's daughter?' The solicitor had agreed to meet Inspector Kershaw for a quick lunch and, in addition to handing over the tape, had elaborated on the interview.

'Yes, she is Ralph's daughter. We had the records checked and have a copy of the birth certificate she gave you,' said Kershaw.

'Did you know she's been to the house or rather, seen it?'

'No, but I've had no occasion to question her regarding that.'

'I hate to agree with her on principle but she's right: that house would probably fetch a good price, if sold.' Peter ate some of his quiche and continued. 'I daresay there's some collectors around who would love to own some of that furniture. It's not to my taste, but Elspeth has made sure it's all in good condition.' And without pausing for breath, 'Any news from forensics?'

'No, but I'm hoping to have the results later today. However, when do you intend to tell Isabel and Elspeth about Marina?'

'This afternoon. As soon as Marina left I rearranged two appointments and phoned Isabel. I realise they'll be shocked, want proof, so I'm taking a photocopy of the birth certificate, Marina's passport and one of Ralph's letters.'

The two men ate in silence then it was Peter who spoke again. 'You're probably thinking the same as me, that if Marina is in any way responsible for Ralph's death, she couldn't benefit from his estate. However, I must advise them of her existence.'

Kershaw nodded. 'I've spoken to the two men I met briefly at Ralph's funeral. Their names were on the list supplied by the funeral director. They were at the College of Further Education in Bournemouth at the same time as Ralph. After prompting, they both remembered Felicity Bushell. One described her as a pretty young woman who worked in the bursar's office while the other said her parents were a charming friendly couple who lived on the outskirts of town.

However, neither had ever seen Ralph with her or any other female, but this did not deter our enquiries. Having acquired the Bushells' address, we learnt from elderly neighbours that Felicity, together with her daughter, had lived with her parents until they moved into a residential home. The old man remembered that the grandparents had been very kind to the little girl – it was a pity her father had died when she was a baby.'

'I suppose that was the best story to tell the neighbours and anyone else,' said Peter. 'So it sounds as though Marina is who she says she is.'

'Unfortunately, the officer didn't have a photograph, but they described the child as having brown hair and dark brown eyes.' Kershaw noted that Peter had finished his quiche, asked the waitress to bring two coffees and resumed, 'I'm sorry Isabel is going to have another shock. There seems to be one thing after the other happening in that household.'

'Marina may not find it as easy as she thinks. I'm dealing with Ralph's estate, looking after Isabel's and Elspeth's interests so, dependent on their reaction and what you learn this afternoon, it may be necessary for Marina to find someone else to act on her behalf.' Peter paused as coffee was placed before him, and when the waitress moved away, 'As I said before, that young woman is very determined to get her hands on Ralph's money.'

Kershaw held his breath. Peter had been very co-operative and already knew about the expected call from forensics, but Kershaw considered this was not the moment to tell him that on the Saturday afternoon Ralph had died there had been three sightings of a person wearing an Austrian-styled coat walking along the road where Kieran and Marina lived.

Although it was only a short time since he had lunched with the inspector, Peter accepted a cup of tea and glancing at Isabel and Elspeth, he said, 'I'm afraid I have some news which will come as rather a shock.'

'Is there something wrong with Ralph's will?' asked Isabel.

'No, not exactly.' Peter hesitated; he had never found himself in such a delicate situation and struggled to find the right words.

Elspeth leant forward and, almost as though she was reading his thoughts, she asked, 'Is there someone claiming against his estate?'

'One of his pupils?' hazarded Isabel.

'Yes, there is a claimant but not a pupil.' Peter looked from one to the other and then, emboldened, 'It's his daughter – his illegitimate daughter.'

'What!' exclaimed Isabel and Elspeth together and then the latter said, 'It's impossible.'

'What do you mean?' asked Peter, thinking she was about to tell him that Ralph was impotent or, for some reason, had had a vasectomy. That would certainly upset Marina.

'I've never known him to look at a girl or young woman until he met Isabel again. I can't imagine…' Elspeth's voice faded and she looked across at Isabel, 'Are you all right?'

'Yes, it's just the shock.'

'Her name is Marina Bushell,' offered Peter.

'Marina Bushell!' echoed Isabel. 'Unless there's someone else of that name, I've met her.'

'What!' exclaimed Elspeth while Peter looked perplexed.

Isabel resumed. 'She's Kieran O'Brien's partner. She was there, at that dinner party.'

'When you…' Elspeth's voice had become a whisper and she glanced at Peter who knew Isabel had been very ill, and who now resumed, 'She's twenty-seven.'

Peter noticed Elspeth's raised eyebrows but continued, 'She produced her birth certificate on which Ralph is named as her father. Normally, if a child is born out of wedlock, the father's name doesn't appear. However, Ralph said in one of the two letters that he wrote to Felicity, Marina's mother, and which Marina also produced, that he was agreeable to his name appearing.'

'Felicity Bushell.' Elspeth shook her head. 'Even though it's a long time ago, I've never heard of anyone of that name,' and glancing at Isabel, 'have you?'

'No. I'm still flabbergasted,' then, turning to Peter, 'Marina's been in Bristol for six years and, while it would have been a shock to all of us, why didn't she make an attempt to see Ralph before he became so ill?'

'She said she was apprehensive.'

'But she's not apprehensive about claiming against the estate,' retorted Elspeth.

'Marina certainly wasn't very happy when she left my office. I told her that if she intended to claim against Ralph's estate she would have to find someone else to act for her.' Peter omitted to say that he had refused Marina's request for what he considered to be an outrageous advance and, in view of her statement that the house was probably worth a fortune, considered her mercenary and a liar.

'Do you think Marina will come here, want to see us?' Isabel looked at Elspeth as she closed the front door behind Peter Hoskins.

'Why should she? Marina has already met you, although she didn't make herself known as Ralph's daughter.'

'She might want to meet you. You're her aunt, her closest and only relative.' They were now back in the lounge, sitting in the two shabby armchairs.

'I hadn't thought of that, but the fact that she didn't attempt to make herself known while Ralph was alive doesn't endear her to me.' Elspeth looked thoughtful. 'As we've said before, so much has happened in a comparatively short time. Ralph died, you suffered from food poisoning and there were those attacks on Duncan but no one has been arrested.' Elspeth paused but only for a moment. 'Damn it, it's three weeks since that dinner party. It must have been Kieran or Marina, so why are the police taking so long?'

'I'm sure the inspector is doing his best.'

The front door opened and closed while Isabel was speaking and, as he stood in the doorway, Duncan asked, 'What's the matter?' Duncan knew about Hoskins' visit and glancing from one to the other, 'Has something else happened?'

Isabel and Elspeth looked at each other and, without prompting, said simultaneously, 'You tell Duncan!'

'Marina, Kieran's partner, is Ralph's illegitimate daughter and she intends to claim against his estate,' echoed Duncan five minutes later. 'Is she likely to come here?' Then, before either could comment, 'I'm going to phone the inspector.'

Inspector Kershaw replaced the receiver and, aware of Tom's undisguised curiosity, summarised the conversation with Kieran and concluded, 'O'Brien's really worried about Marina.'

'But he knows she was taking a party of Germans to the Cotswolds,' said Tom. 'I'm surprised she didn't phone him during the lunch break.'

Kershaw nodded then recalled Hoskins' comment, 'She's a liar', which referred to Marina's remark that the house should be worth a fortune. Hoskins' next comment, 'She's greedy', had been explained by Marina's request for £5,000. The solicitor had said that Marina's expression changed yet again when he told her that he would have to inform Isabel and Elspeth and that he would be in touch. Her reply had been abrupt and she had departed in a bad temper.

Kershaw glanced at his watch, wondered how Isabel and Elspeth were reacting and if Peter Hoskins was still with them. He considered that this case was becoming more involved, and he certainly didn't want any more complications. There was only one sensible way to find out: ring Peter, but he would give him a little longer to return to his office.

Fifteen minutes later, Kershaw learnt that Isabel and Elspeth were shocked and that Isabel had immediately realised she had met Marina at the dinner party.

'Were they alone when you left? And although she should be with a party of Germans, was there any sign of Marina in the vicinity?' asked Kershaw.

'Duncan had gone to the library, but he's probably back by now, and I'm glad to say there was no sign of that unpleasant young woman. I certainly didn't tell Isabel and Elspeth that Marina was in an aggressive and bad-tempered mood when she left.'

'They should be all right if Duncan's there and Marina does call,' said Kershaw.

'Surely you don't think that Marina would call at the house and do something stupid?'

'I think that young woman is capable...' Kershaw stopped abruptly, then reached for the handset Tom was holding, saying, 'Duncan's on the other line. I'll speak to you later.'

'Did you know that Peter Hoskins was going to call on Isabel, and the reason for his visit?' demanded Duncan and before Kershaw could reply, 'How long have you known that Marina was Ralph's daughter? When did you find out? Surely you could have warned Isabel?' and, without pausing for breath, 'To think we went to that dinner party and Marina never gave any indication. She must be a cold-hearted bitch!'

Kershaw took advantage of the pause to remind Duncan that Hoskins was dealing with Ralph's estate but was unprepared as Duncan's tirade continued: 'I'm amazed that Hoskins could calmly deliver this news and then leave them alone in the house.'

'I'm sure they're both very–'

'If Marina's determined to get her hands on Ralph's money, there's no knowing what that young woman might do,' interrupted Duncan. 'No doubt Kieran is still at the hotel, but do you know where she is? Have you any idea what she's likely to do if her claim isn't recognised?'

'Please, Mr Sinclair, calm down.' Kershaw wondered if Isabel or Elspeth could hear Duncan and resumed, 'Your attitude isn't helping anyone.'

'I'm sorry, Inspector. I got carried away. So much has happened and now this – to learn that Ralph had an illegitimate daughter.'

'I agree; it is a shock, and while I doubt that Marina will do anything untoward, why don't you stay with Isabel and Elspeth for a couple of nights?'

Kershaw heard Duncan give a deep sigh of relief and then, 'Thank you for that suggestion, Inspector. I'm probably behaving like a fool, but I'd never forgive myself if anything happened.'

'Sinclair certainly got you rattled. What was it all about?' asked Tom as Kershaw gratefully sank into his chair.

'Hoskins' visit and Marina. Could you organise some tea please, and I'll tell you.'

'Will you arrange for someone to check the McGuire neighbourhood around the time that Marina's due to finish her escort duties?' asked Tom after he had heard of Duncan's concern for Isabel and Elspeth.

Kershaw looked thoughtful. 'Although we know Duncan will be in the house, it might be a good idea to have someone there, but not Sergeant Lovell. Marina would probably recognise her.'

19

Marina sat behind the driver talking to the youngest member of the German party, still amazed that so much had happened in such a short time.

The minibus had been parked outside, and a group of men were standing in the foyer when she arrived at the hotel that morning. As she approached, one of them detached himself from the group, came towards her and took her hands in his exclaiming, 'Marina! How marvellous to see you!'

The moment she looked into Fritz's deep blue eyes she had felt herself trembling as she remembered the many happy hours they had spent together whenever she had been staying in his parents' hotel. This was situated near Lake Constance and she had been a courier in charge of a party of holiday-makers. At the time, she knew that Fritz was engaged, but she now noticed that he was not wearing a wedding ring; however, this was not always significant. The other men, all considerably older, had smiled and nodded with approval as he kissed her on both cheeks and taken it for granted that the young couple would sit together.

In spite of the emotional turmoil which overwhelmed her, Marina had pointed out familiar landscapes then, as they drove into the country, left the older men to enjoy the picturesque villages, some very tiny, the golden-stoned houses and cottages. This was achieved by turning off main roads and negotiating narrow lanes but Adam, the driver, was accustomed to this.

Fritz had taken this opportunity to whisper that, much to his parents' disapproval, he had broken off his engagement and waited patiently for Marina's next visit but this did not happen. Unfortunately, he did not have her home address and, after discreet enquiries, he had been bitterly disappointed to learn that the travel agents for whom Marina had worked would no longer be sending groups to his parents' or any other hotel in that town.

During their coffee break when, much to the others' amusement, he had manoeuvred her towards a table for two, she had agreed to spend the evening with him, saying she would have to go home to change. Fritz had then pointed out that this was unnecessary; there were probably shops or a boutique at wherever they were stopping for lunch when they could buy a dress and whatever else she needed. He was sure the older men, who had appreciated the brief stops in order that they could take photographs, would be happy to spend some time on their own. It would give them an opportunity to buy postcards and possibly souvenirs for their families.

After lunch, which was enjoyed at the leading hotel in the centre of the village of Broadway, Fritz had seen and swept her into a smart boutique where he insisted that she try on the stunning black cocktail dress which was in the window. This had been a perfect fit and, to her amazement, he had chosen matching lingerie and high-heeled sandals.

Back in the minibus, the afternoon passed swiftly, their first brief stop being at Stow-on-the-Wold where the Germans had been intrigued at the number of antique shops and narrow streets. At Bibury, some had admired Arlington Row – a row of charming cottages – or the Swan Hotel, while others had visited the church.

It was some time later that Fritz had whispered, 'Where shall we spend the night? I'm sure you don't want to stay at my hotel,' and, as she hesitated, 'if you'd prefer somewhere out of town but are worried about getting in for work tomorrow, that's no problem. I'll have to come back myself and we can easily organise a taxi.'

Delighted that Fritz, now an affluent hotelier and, to her astonishment, unmarried, should suddenly appear claiming that he was still in love with her, Marina named two hotels on the outskirts of Bristol.

She was even more amazed when he produced a list of Bristol hotels, studied this and then took his mobile from his pocket. A few seconds later, he told her, 'That's all arranged.'

It was as Fritz replaced his mobile that Marina suddenly realised she hadn't phoned or even thought about Kieran and quickly decided that, although he would be annoyed, she would phone him after the tour. She would tell him that she was spending the evening with one of the girls from the agency who had suggested that, instead of returning to Henleaze, she should stay the night. Dimly, she heard Fritz say, 'We're going to have a marvellous time.'

Detective Sergeant Tom Small looked up expectantly every time the phone rang on the inspector's desk, but it was mid-afternoon when it rang yet again. Kershaw's voice changed and Tom was pleased to see him smiling. The conversation was brief and Kershaw concluded, 'I look forward to receiving your fax.' Then, looking at Tom, 'It's amazing what forensics can find. The hairs from Marina's brush and comb match those on the coat, the fibres on Ralph's bedspread were from Stefan Baumgarten's coat, and the tissue that he found in his pocket was the same as those in the packet Rowena found with Marina's other toiletries. And we already know why that particular tissue was used.'

'So we can now bring Marina in for further questioning.' Tom hesitated. 'But she's probably still working.'

'In which case, we'll see Mrs Cole and then go on to Henleaze.' Tom and Detective Sergeant Rowena Lovell had called at the flat on Saturday morning when they learnt that Eunice was spending the weekend in Weston-super-Mare.

The first-floor tenant informed them that Eunice would be returning Monday afternoon.

Detective Sergeant Norman Quigley had already seen the photograph taken by Tom and observed that Marina looked very different, pointing out that she had been wearing a courier's uniform when the original photo was taken.

At the time he saw her in Whiteladies Road, standing behind Duncan, her gloved hand on his back, she was wearing a nondescript tracksuit. He had noted her height and dark hair which, although he only caught a glimpse of her profile, was sufficient for him to say that she was the same person. Quigley had again apologised that he had not run after her; he had been more concerned about Duncan.

Kershaw stood up and tore off the sheet of paper which had just emerged from the fax machine, studied this, nodded, and handed it to Tom with the comment, 'Marvellous what modern technology can do.'

'Do you think Kieran knows that Marina borrowed Stefan's coat and could be responsible for Ralph McGuire's death?' asked Tom a few minutes later, as they fastened their seat belts.

'No, but he certainly sounded very concerned about her.'

Kershaw had been surprised to receive a phone call from Kieran late that morning when he recounted Marina's admission that she was Ralph's illegitimate daughter and that she had not phoned him, as promised, after her visit to the solicitor. He recalled the urgency in Kieran's voice: 'She doesn't answer her mobile which I know she usually keeps switched on, even when working.'

Kershaw had learnt that Marina was due to meet a party of Germans after her appointment with Hoskins and, according to the agency, there had been no complaints that this excursion was not proceeding as planned. He had then suggested that Marina might phone during her lunch break, but when Kieran had phoned again at half past two, he had still not heard from Marina and sounded even more agitated. 'I'm worried, concerned that if the interview with the solicitor didn't go as she hoped, she might do something silly.'

Kershaw's comment that she was obviously with the

German party was quickly interrupted with, 'Marina was so determined that she should inherit a substantial legacy, she might think of going to see Mrs. McGuire, possibly when she returns this afternoon. That would be a terrible shock for Isabel who I thought was a very charming person. If I can't contact Marina, how can I stop her?'

'I'm sure you're worrying unnecessarily, Mr O'Brien.'

Kershaw decided there was no need to inform Kieran of Hoskins' visit to the McGuire household and continued: 'Marina will probably come home at her usual time and apologise that she was too busy to phone you.'

'I hope so. We don't usually have long together then. Sometimes she doesn't get in until half past five and I like to be back at the hotel by six o'clock.'

'So he'll be in for a shock when we arrive,' said Tom.

'How can I help you, Inspector?' Eunice Cole had apologised that she couldn't see them earlier, poured tea and indicated slices of a delicious-looking sponge.

'My niece made that this morning.'

'It's about the afternoon you met Duncan Sinclair. I realise that's ten days ago; however, I'm wondering if you recognise this young lady.' Kershaw placed the photograph of Marina on the table and continued: 'I doubt she was wearing that uniform.'

'Imagine her in casual clothes,' suggested Tom. He had just helped himself to a slice of sponge and now bit into this, his eyes lighting up with obvious enjoyment.

Eunice looked thoughtful. 'As I told that nice Mr Sinclair, there were several people all around me and I couldn't see exactly who was behind him.' Eunice drank some of her tea, studied the photograph again and then said, 'I'll just close my eyes and think.'

'Take your time.' Kershaw's gaze travelled around the room, from the tiny white-haired woman sat opposite him to the small dining table and four chairs in a corner, to a small bookcase where he noted several of Duncan's books. Although slightly faded, the patterned carpet and plain curtains were clean, and all the furniture highly polished.

Aware of a slight movement, he looked at Eunice who said, 'I think there were three people between me and the road.' Then looking at the photo once more, 'She's a tall young woman and there was a tallish person in front of the young boy who was in front of me. But I did notice that this person was wearing a grey tracksuit which looked rather scruffy. The hood, which had been pulled up, fell back and the hair, which was slicked back, was dark. I couldn't tell whether it was a man or woman. You can't these days, some men have long hair and…'

'Did you see her face?'

'No, I'm afraid I didn't. There was such a rush to cross. It's amazing Mr Sinclair didn't fall, but he did look dazed when I reached the edge of the pavement.

From the way he spoke, I thought that he and this other person were together. Everyone who had crossed was going in different directions and I don't remember seeing anyone in a scruffy tracksuit on the opposite pavement. She could have turned back in the scramble, got caught up with those who came from the other side – that often happens – and walked up towards Whiteladies Road.'

Kershaw noticed that, although he was taking notes, Tom glanced up and considered that they were both probably thinking the same thing: Quigley had suggested that Marina could have been heading for Blackboy Hill.

'Why should Marina, if it is her, threaten Duncan about the biography and want to harm him? What would she gain?' asked Tom some ten minutes later, as he drove across the Downs, towards Henleaze.

'Perhaps she thinks that if anything happened to Isabel he would inherit some of the money left to her by Ralph.'

'According to Belinda Baumgarten, he was very attentive towards Isabel during the dinner party,' said Tom.

'That's not surprising. It was the first time she had been out since Ralph's death. And don't forget, they knew each other years ago. Elspeth told me, in confidence, that Duncan's mother died suddenly, leaving him with the responsibility of caring for a physically handicapped younger sister.'

'I wonder if he and Isabel will eventually get together again?' hazarded Tom.

Inspector Kershaw and Tom both took a step backwards as the front door was flung open. Kieran snapped, 'Where's your key?' and then apologised. 'I'm sorry, Inspector, I thought you were Marina. However, please come in.' Then, as they all stood in the hall, 'I haven't heard from Marina. Her mobile is still switched off and, as you can guess, I'm angry and frustrated. She knows I'm due back at the hotel. I don't know how she can be so inconsiderate.'

'Perhaps something unexpected has occurred,' offered Kershaw.

'I phoned the agency ten minutes ago. There hasn't been an accident or breakdown.' Then, glancing from one to the other, 'Why are you here? Has there been an accident?'

'No, we want to talk to Marina.'

At that moment, the phone rang. Kieran grabbed the receiver and, unable to control his frustration, demanded, 'Marina, where are you? I've been frantic with worry – you promised to phone and I couldn't ring you. Your mobile's been switched off all day.'

Kieran's expression changed from one of concern to bewilderment. 'This is very sudden. You're usually talking about a girls' night out days beforehand, and I've never known you to stay with anyone.' Kershaw and Tom watched as Kieran shook the receiver. 'Damn it, she's rung off.' After he had attempted, unsuccessfully, to call Marina, he said, 'She's switched off again. What's going on? It doesn't take long to come home and change.'

Kershaw silently agreed, wondering why Marina was acting so strangely – there was no way she could know he was waiting to question her. It was possible she had bought something new to wear this evening, but Kershaw quickly dismissed these thoughts. Marina had been in charge of a party of German businessmen who would probably want her undivided attention all day.

'Ring the agency again,' suggested Tom. 'She might still be there.'

Kieran dialled and when there was no reply Kershaw asked, 'Could you phone her friend?'

'I don't know who it is; she didn't mention anyone by name. I can't understand why she hasn't come home to change or why she didn't say anything last night, or this morning.' Kieran sighed. 'She'll probably turn up tomorrow and say she did tell me, but I know damn well she didn't. And now, if you'll excuse me, I must go. I'm sorry you've had a wasted journey, Inspector.'

It was as he unlocked his car that Kieran glanced at

the two detectives who were standing on the pavement. 'By the way, why do you want to see Marina?' and without waiting for a reply, 'Can I give her a message? Ask her to contact you?'

'No thanks, we'll catch up with her.'

20

'Give me the agency number, please. I'll try it again before we decide on our next move.' Seated in the car outside Kieran's house, Inspector Kershaw was about to give up when a surprised male voice said, 'Hullo, we're closed. There's no one here.'

'I realise that, but who are you?'

'I'm Adam, the minibus driver,' and, sounding belligerent, 'who are you?'

As so often happened, Tom found himself listening to a one-sided conversation and glanced at the inspector as he identified himself and said that he needed to contact Marina Bushell, who had not yet returned home to Henleaze.

'And I don't think she will tonight. She's probably with that German chap – he was the youngest in the group.' Adam's voice was now quite loud; then, as an afterthought, he asked, 'How do I know you're really a inspector? You could be Kieran checking up on her.'

'I'm not O'Brien. I'm with Detective Sergeant Tom Small. You can ring HQ if you want to check on us.'

'I wouldn't do that. I say,' Adam now sounded excited, 'is something exciting happening? Can I help you with your enquiries?' And then, in a rush, 'Marina and this Fritz were sat together, behind me, talking all the time. They certainly weren't strangers. I wasn't eaves... eavesdropping, but I heard him ask her out for dinner. I'm sorry I don't know where they're going.'

'You've been very helpful Mr... Adam. Thank you.'

Kershaw was about to switch off when Adam offered, 'He... this Fritz, was talking about dining at a hotel outside of Bristol, spending the night there, but Marina will be in to work tomorrow morning. We're booked to take another French party to Bath.'

'That's most interesting. Thank you.' Kershaw then learnt that Adam had been standing beside the minibus and the Germans were in the hotel foyer when Marina arrived, that this Fritz chap had immediately come forward to greet her.

'He kissed her on both cheeks,' burbled Adam.

Kershaw grinned. It was obvious this driver was thoroughly enjoying himself then Adam resumed, 'Marina doesn't usually turn up at the pick-up point but apparently she had an early appointment. Whatever it was must have upset her. She looked very annoyed as she approached the bus, but as soon as this Fritz appeared everything about her changed.' Kershaw reached for a pen and pad as Adam said, 'I'll give you my phone number. I'll be home all the evening if you need any more information.'

'So where do we go from here?' asked Tom.

'As far as Marina is concerned, nowhere at the moment. According to Adam, she'll be at the agency before starting off with a party of French teachers. There's no point in contacting Kieran; he's working and thinks Marina is still with a girlfriend.' Kershaw glanced at Tom. 'That's it for today. We'll see Marina first thing in the morning.'

'Perhaps this Fritz will want to take her back to Germany. D'you think she would go?'

'Not until she's got what she considers to be her share of Ralph's estate.' Kershaw paused. 'Hoskins confirms my opinion, that she's a mercenary young woman.'

'What about Quigley? Is he still watching the McGuire household?'

'No. He's been told to return to the station.'

'Why don't you sit down and relax?' Isabel watched as Duncan stood at the window, gazing up and down the road. 'I doubt that Marina would have the nerve to call without phoning.'

'I'm sorry. I didn't mean to upset you. I'm just amazed that you've accepted the news that Ralph had an illegitimate daughter so calmly.' Then, as he crossed the room towards the settee on which Isabel was sitting, Duncan continued: 'I've done some stupid things in my life and leaving you like I did, all those years ago, was the most stupid. I should have told you that my mother had died and, even before that, that I had a younger, physically handicapped sister. Losing my mother so suddenly was a terrible shock to both of us. My sister was devastated and wouldn't let me out of her sight. When Ralph asked me…'

Duncan stopped abruptly as the doorbell rang and gazed at Isabel with tender reassurance, but before he could move he heard a young female voice say, 'Hullo, Aunt Elspeth. How are you? I thought I'd pop in to see how you and Isabel were, and I met this young man on the doorstep.'

At the sound of the male voice, which he instantly recognised, Duncan hurried into the hall. 'Quigley, what are you doing here?'

'The inspector asked me to stay in this area in case Miss Bushell came here after work; however, I've just heard that this is now highly improbable and that I'm to return to the station.' Then, glancing down at Joanna, who was gazing up at him with a bemused expression, 'And I met Miss McGuire.'

'It's very good of you to let us know. Would you like a drink before you go?'

'No thank you, sir. I'm still on duty.'

'I'll see you out,' offered Joanna. As she accompanied the young sergeant to the front door and opened it, Quigley was heard to say, 'Thank you, Miss McGuire,' and in a rush, 'could we meet sometime, for a drink?'

'Yes, I'd like that.' Elspeth and Duncan grinned at each other then quickly composed their features as Joanna, her face slightly flushed, turned and asked, 'Who's this Miss Bushell?'

'Come into the lounge and we'll tell you about it. But before we start, would you like a cup of tea? Can you stay for supper?'

'I'm not bothered about tea but yes, supper would be great.' Joanna glanced at Duncan. 'You're working late.'

'Duncan's staying with us for a couple of days,' said Elspeth.

'What's happened? What's going on?' asked Joanna.

Elspeth gave Joanna a gentle push. 'Go and say hullo to Isabel. I'll join you in a minute.'

Some fifteen minutes later, during which Joanna had uttered comments of surprise and anger, she exclaimed, 'It's incredible!' Then, her head turning as she looked from Elspeth to Isabel, 'You say Uncle Ralph knew about Marina but he never mentioned her existence to either of you?' And when they shook their heads, 'I know he was a strange man, always absorbed in books – other people's and his own – but to ignore her completely, it's… it's inhuman.'

Joanna had also learnt of Hoskins' visit and now asked, 'If Marina knew he was her father and has been in Bristol for the last six years, why didn't she get in touch, come to see him?' But before anyone could reply and looking at Isabel, Joanna resumed, 'You and Duncan met her at that dinner party. What did you think of her? Did she look like Uncle Ralph?'

'She was very pleasant and, no.'

'It's no wonder Kieran has been looking so worried. He's such a nice person, always polite and very capable. All his staff like and respect him, as do the management. I only saw him for a few moments before I left, when he seemed even more worried.'

'He's probably concerned about Marina's strange behaviour. Apparently, she didn't phone him, as promised, after she'd seen Hoskins,' offered Duncan, who had learnt this from his conversation with Kershaw.

It was later, as they all sat around the kitchen table eating shepherd's pie, carrots and peas that Joanna suddenly said, 'It's all my fault. I should never have allowed Marina in.'

'You didn't. Mr Gresham, from opposite, saw her push the door open and barge in,' said Isabel. 'And she went straight up to Uncle's room, almost as though she had been there before. But she hadn't, had she?' asked Joanna

'No,' chorused Isabel and Elspeth.

'It must have been her that gave Uncle all those

tablets. He was all right before she arrived, a bit crotchety but that's nothing new. I know he was ill and extremely awkward, that he could hardly speak and everything was getting more difficult for you. But why did she wait so long?' And when there was no reply: 'So now she intends to claim…' Joanna stopped abruptly, looking thoughtful and then resumed, 'If the police have evidence that Marina was responsible for Uncle's death she wouldn't be allowed to benefit.'

Joanna ate the remainder of the shepherd's pie that was on her plate. 'That was delicious,' then, looking at Isabel, 'It must have been Kieran or Marina who poisoned your food at that dinner party. Have the police found out who was responsible, and what are they doing about it?' Barely pausing for breath, Joanna turned to Duncan. 'How do you know Sergeant Quigley and why are you staying here?'

'Really, Joanna; I'm sure Isabel and Duncan don't want to go over all this again,' remonstrated Elspeth.

'It's all right,' said Isabel. 'Although you've phoned, we haven't seen you since I came out of hospital. You're part of the family and it's understandable you want to know what's been happening. Duncan can tell you.'

Isabel glanced at Duncan who nodded and quickly told Joanna about the berries from the laburnum tree, threatening phone calls and attempts to push him off the pavement. 'Sergeant Quigley rescued me the second time and our only regret is that by him doing so, the perpetrator got away.'

'He seems rather nice, the sergeant, I mean.'

Joanna looked thoughtful for a moment and then asked, 'Was it the same person on both occasions? Have you any idea who it was?' Then, before Duncan could reply: 'Are you staying here because this person is watching your flat?'

'Good heavens, no!' exclaimed Duncan. 'On learning that Marina left Hoskins' office in a bad temper, I was concerned that she might come round here and create a fuss. However, you heard what Sergeant Quigley says, so we can all relax.'

'But where is Marina? What's going to happen now?'

'Now I've found you, I don't intend to lose you again.'

Fritz spoke quietly as he gazed at Marina across the candle-lit table. 'Come back to Germany with me.'

Marina gazed back at Fritz, revelling in the luxury of the elegant dining room and the attentiveness of the *maitre d'hotel* and waiters. She had been thrilled to discover a bottle of champagne in their suite and forgot everything else as Fritz gathered her in his arms, kissing and caressing her, at the same time removing her clothes. His sensuality and passion were as intense as when she first met him, and now she was overwhelmed by the ardour in his voice. Although Fritz had said he was still in love with her, he hadn't mentioned marriage and, shaking her head, she told him, 'It's not as simple as that.'

'You mean you ARE married to this Kieran? Or to someone else before you moved in with him?'

'No, it's to do with my father.'

'Bring him to Germany.'

'He's dead,' and before Fritz could speak, 'it's rather complicated, but I'll try to tell you as quickly as I can.'

Fritz listened as Marina, pausing only when their plates were removed and the main course served, told him that she was the illegitimate daughter of Ralph McGuire who had recently died, and that she intended to claim against his estate.

'There's no need for you to do that. I can take care of you.'

Marina ignored this. She knew that in addition to the hotel Fritz had inherited from his parents, he now owned another hotel in the same area, and continued: 'Although he acknowledged that he was my father – his name appears on my birth certificate – he completely ignored my mother and I. His wife (who he married years later) and sister live in a large house which, together with the contents, must be worth a fortune. It's only fair that I should have something,' then, realising this sounded a bit mercenary, 'tell me more about your life in Germany.'

Marina already knew that there was a capable young manager in charge of each hotel but, despite this, Fritz checked daily that his high standards were maintained. She was sure that, as his wife, she would achieve the lifestyle which she had always craved, but first she must acquire her share of Ralph's estate. However, in the meantime, as she enjoyed the delicious fillet steak, she learnt about his newly built house and holidays to exotic destinations.

At the same time that Marina and Fritz were studying the sweet menu, Stefan Baumgarten was spooning sugar into his coffee but looking at Kieran with concern then, calling the waiter who was re-laying an adjacent table, told him, 'Take my coffee to my office please, George.' The young waiter nodded, placed the cup and saucer on a small tray while Stefan rose to his feet and approached Kieran. 'Can you spare a few minutes?'

'Is anything wrong, Mr Baumgarten?' enquired Kieran as he stood just inside the general manager's office.

'No, certainly not with the hotel or me, but what's troubling you, Kieran? Are you ill or is it a problem you'd like to discuss?'

'I'm sorry; I shouldn't bring my problems to work.' Kieran hesitated and then, 'I don't really know if it's Marina or me. I don't understand her or the way she's behaving.'

'Come and sit down,' invited Stefan, pulling

another chair alongside his, behind the desk. 'Is Marina still unhappy, dissatisfied?'

'There's more to it than that.' Kieran looked thoughtful then quickly told Stefan what he had learnt on Sunday and that Marina had visited Ralph's solicitor that morning. 'She promised to phone me, to let me know what happened. I know she was working, but they always have a coffee and lunch break, and she takes her mobile with her. She didn't phone until I was about to leave home this evening and then told me she was going out with one of the girls from the agency and would be spending the night at her place. Marina didn't mention what had happened with this Mr Hoskins, just rang off abruptly. And that's another thing: the inspector and his sergeant were there at the time, wanting to see her. But they didn't tell me why.'

Stefan wondered if Kershaw had heard from forensics, if the hairs on his coat had been identified as belonging to Marina and what was going to happen. Then, looking at Kieran's pale face and creased brow, he asked, 'Was Marina very fond of her father, upset when he died?'

'Although she's lived in Bristol for six years, she's never met him.'

'But she thinks she's entitled to part of his estate?'

'Oh yes,' and although he knew it sounded disloyal, Kieran found himself saying, 'she's most determined about it – asserts that he ignored her and her mother. Inspector Kershaw said he'd catch up with her tomorrow but didn't clarify if he means to be at the agency first thing in the morning.'

'I know this sounds trite, but try not to worry. I'm sure Marina is capable of answering whatever questions he asks,' said Stefan.

21

In spite of a restless night, Joanna arrived at the hotel very early and, although surprised, the night duty manager greeted her in his usual amicable manner, assuring her that everything was in order.

Joanna was about to turn away from Reception when she heard Kieran speak and, turning, immediately noticed the dark shadows under his eyes. Recalling the lengthy conversation about Marina that had taken place during and after supper the previous evening, Joanna guessed that, while she had been concerned about Isabel, Kieran had probably spent a sleepless night worried about Marina. 'How are you?' she asked, at the same time that Kieran asked, 'How is Isabel?'

'Fine. In fact, I had supper and spent the evening with them.'

'Then you...' Kieran stopped abruptly and Joanna said quickly, 'Neither of us are due on duty yet. Let's go and have a coffee, maybe something to eat, in the staff dining room.'

'I expect you know that Marina was Ralph

McGuire's illegitimate daughter,' said Kieran some ten minutes later as they sat opposite each other and when Joanna nodded: 'I only heard about it on Sunday.'

Joanna gazed at Kieran, amazed. 'Marina hadn't told you? Even though you've been together for six years.'

'She obviously didn't think it was important.'

Kieran helped himself to a slice of toast, buttered and cut it in half. 'She also told me she was going to see Ralph's solicitor. Her appointment was yesterday morning before accompanying a party of German businessmen on a tour of the Cotswolds; however, I haven't seen her since. She promised to let me know the outcome of that interview, but she didn't phone until I was about to leave for work. She then told me she was going out with one of the girls from the agency and would be spending the night at her friend's place. She didn't say anything about the interview.'

'Didn't she come home to change?'

'No, which was most unusual. She always likes to get out of her uniform.'

Joanna nodded and reflected that Marina had probably decided she needed a night out. She had obviously gone straight from the solicitor's office to the hotel where she was to meet the German party, but why didn't she phone Kieran? There must have been ample opportunity. What had happened during the day to make her so thoughtless?

Suppressing these thoughts, Joanna said, 'I suppose you went home and spent the rest of the evening worrying about her?'

'Not exactly,' Kieran grinned. 'It was almost as though Zak knew I needed company. He rang me immediately after the play finished and asked if he could come round, which he did. We had a few drinks when he told me about his role in the new production and some amusing anecdotes about some of his fellow actors.

'I felt much better when he left, but this morning I was worried about Marina again.'

'I'm sure she'll soon be in touch with an acceptable explanation,' then glancing at her watch, Joanna said, 'duty calls. Let me know if you want to talk about Marina, or there's anything I can do.'

Marina glanced out of the window to see Inspector Kershaw and Detective Sergeant Small approach her taxi as it stopped outside the escort agency. Immediately, she leant forward. 'I don't want to stop here. Drive on and I'll tell you where I want to go.'

'I was only paid to bring you here,' replied the driver.

'Don't worry. I'll pay you the extra.' Her thoughts confused, Marina fumbled with the zip of her bag. Why were the inspector and his sergeant waiting for her? But more importantly, where did she want to go? For the last twelve hours she had enjoyed Fritz's company and revelled in his lovemaking, but now she suddenly recalled her unsuccessful interview with Mr Hoskins and muttered under her breath, 'Why should Isabel and Elspeth inherit everything?' Then, without thinking what she intended to say or do when she got there, she gave the driver the McGuire address.

'Those two men who were on the pavement outside the agency are in a car immediately behind us,' said the driver as he drove along Park Row, already indicating that he intended to turn left at the Victoria Rooms.

At this, Marina leant forward again. 'I've changed my mind. I don't want to go to that address in Clifton. Take me to Henleaze.'

'For Christ's sake, make up your mind,' muttered the driver.

'What's she playing at?' asked Tom and swore as the taxi driver suddenly changed direction, driving straight ahead along Whiteladies Road.

'Just keep following her,' instructed Kershaw.

'That car is still behind us,' said the taxi driver twenty minutes later as he drew up outside Kieran's house and Marina reached across to pay him. 'They look rather suspicious. Would you like me to phone the police?'

Marina opened the door, swung her legs to the ground and stood on the pavement. 'They are the police,' she told him. 'An inspector and his sergeant.'

'My God! Have I been aiding and abetting a criminal? I picked you up from a posh hotel and some foreign bloke paid your fare.'

But Marina wasn't listening. She had already unlocked the front door while the inspector was immediately behind her and Detective Sergeant Small was questioning the taxi driver.

'Good Morning, Miss Bushell,' said Kershaw. 'We need to ask you a few questions. Unfortunately, we couldn't find you yesterday evening. However, now will suit us.'

'It's not really convenient. I'm due to take a party of French teachers to Bath.'

'Now? Surely it's rather early.'

'How long will this take?'

'That depends on you. How co-operative you are.'

'Then it won't take long.' Marina looked at Detective Sergeant Small as he came into the hall and nodded at the inspector then she pushed open the lounge door and preceded the two men into the room. It was as she indicated chairs that Marina noticed Tom had a dark green coat over his arm and was carrying a wide-brimmed hat, and asked, 'What are you doing with those?'

Tom laid the coat across the back of a chair and

placed the hat on the seat while, still standing, Kershaw asked, 'Do you recognise those garments?'

'I'm sure there are a lot of people who buy clothes like that while on holiday in Austria.'

'That's not what I mean. Stop prevaricating and answer my question, please.'

In spite of Kershaw's persistence, Marina hesitated. 'I think Mr Baumgarten, our neighbour, has a coat and hat like that.'

'I suggest you omit "I think" from that statement. You were seen leaving this house and walking towards the Downs wearing these garments. You were also seen in the Clifton area, approaching and, in fact, entering the McGuire household on the Saturday afternoon that Ralph McGuire died.' As Marina gasped and her eyes widened, Kershaw continued: 'Strands of hair that were found on the collar of the coat and in the hat have been identified as yours.'

'That's ridiculous. Why would I be wearing those garments; and what would I be doing in the McGuire household?'

'I think you know very well what you were doing there. Ralph McGuire was your father and you were probably the last person to see him alive. While you may have been a regular visitor, I'm sure he was delighted to see you again,' and when there was no response, 'or was that the first time you visited him? In which case, he must have been surprised. What did he say?'

Marina shook her head, remembering the only

occasion she had seen the man she knew to be her father, and his attempt to speak – his mouth opening and closing but no sound. Her mind closed to what happened after that and she snapped, 'You've no right to question me like this.'

'But you were there that afternoon. Miniscule fibres from this coat were found on Ralph's bedspread. I must say I find it strange that you should have used Mr Baumgarten's coat, scarf and hat to disguise yourself. It's not the usual thing to do when you visit a sick—'

'Stop it, stop it,' shouted Marina.

'Why don't we all sit down and relax,' suggested Kershaw and, glancing at Tom, 'would you make us some coffee, please?' Then turning back to Marina: 'You only spent a few minutes with your father. Was he still alive when you left?'

'Of course he was. Leaning against his pillows.'

'Exactly as you found him when you arrived?'

Although Marina agreed, Kershaw recalled finding Ralph lying on his back, two pillows on the floor. 'Did he lean forward when you gave him a drink?'

'Yes.' Marina stopped abruptly. 'How do you know about that?'

'You washed the glass but your fingerprints were on the bottle of lemon barley.'

'So I gave him a drink,' retorted Marina. 'There's nothing wrong with that, is there?'

'But it wasn't just lemon barley, was it?'

'What do you mean?'

'The bottle containing his medication was empty.' Kershaw recalled his surprise when Dr Beresford told him of the drug prescribed for Ralph McGuire.

'There was probably another one somewhere else, or Isabel was fetching some more,' said Marina.

Kershaw knew that all the tablets had been used and that there were approximately fifteen in the bottle. He had questioned Isabel and Elspeth about this at the time of Ralph's death and on other occasions. He had guessed and now knew that these had been placed and crushed between a tissue. This had been found in Stefan Baumgarten's coat pocket and examined by forensics, and traces of the granules, which had been tipped into the drink, were discovered embedded in the tissue. Tiny grains had also been found sticking to the handle of the toothbrush which had obviously been used to stir the mixture.

'Did you enjoy yourself last night? I've never eaten at that hotel, but I understand the food is excellent.'

'What are you talking about?'

'The hotel where you stayed last night. I'm sure, as a hotelier, your friend Fritz Hauser was very impressed.'

For a moment, Marina was remembering the champagne and the luxury of the suite they occupied and, without thinking, murmured, 'Yes, he was.' Then she stopped abruptly. 'How do you know all this?' and when reminded that the inspector had been looking for her the previous evening, Marina demanded, 'who told you that?'

Kershaw ignored that and resumed, 'Having disposed of your father, you then poisoned Isabel. You've already denied picking flowers and pods off the laburnum tree in the Baumgartens' garden, but you were seen doing this.'

'Bloody neighbours! Why can't they mind their own business?' exclaimed Marina.

Kershaw ignored this outburst and continued: 'At that time you probably didn't know of Elspeth's existence, so I suppose you hoped that you would inherit everything. But why did you attack Duncan Sinclair? Were you afraid that Isabel would leave him her share of Ralph's estate?' As Marina gasped in astonishment, Kershaw realised the extent of her greed and persisted, 'I suppose you thought the references to the biography would be an adequate distraction.'

'I really don't know what you are talking about.' Marina rose to her feet with an aplomb that Kershaw could not help but admire, and her voice was still steady. 'I refuse to answer any more questions unless a solicitor is present. However, I must get back to the agency. My French party will be waiting for me.'

'I don't think so. Someone else is looking after them and, as far as a solicitor is concerned, you don't need one yet.' And when Marina started to protest, Kershaw's voice became grim. 'I suggest you sit down again, Miss Bushell. There are still a number of questions to be answered. What did Ralph McGuire say when you arrived? When you told him that you were his daughter? Was he surprised, pleased, shocked?'

On learning that Ralph was unable to speak, even mumble, Kershaw felt a pang of sympathy that such an intelligent man had been unable to communicate or move. He knew that Ralph had become angry and bad-tempered when told that his condition would deteriorate but, according to Isabel and Elspeth, and also Dr Beresford, Ralph had insisted that he didn't want any more nurses, or hospitalisation. His views on euthanasia were well-known, but perhaps seeing him so helpless had driven Marina into taking such action.

'He… he looked so old. He couldn't speak. It was terrible,' repeated Marina.

'So you thought you would take matters into your own hands.' Aware of unexpected movement, Kershaw turned quickly to see Kieran standing in the doorway.

'Marina, what are you doing here at this time of the morning? Why aren't you at work?' asked Kieran.

'I could ask you the same question, Mr O'Brien,' said Kershaw and, noting the well-groomed young man standing just behind Kieran, assumed him to be Fritz Hauser while Marina was gazing at one then the other, speechless.

Kieran looked directly at the inspector. 'I was still concerned about Marina, so I phoned the agency to learn that she had arrived by taxi which immediately drove off again, with her still in it. Also, that the two men who had been waiting outside, who answered your description, followed her. Mr Baumgarten could see that I was agitated and suggested I came home for a while. I'll just make myself some coffee.'

As he turned, Kieran looked at Fritz and jerking his head towards the inspector, asked, 'Are you with them?'

'No! I came because Marina left…'

'What! Who are you?' and turning to Marina, Kieran demanded, 'What's going on?'

'Fritz is …'

'That's enough,' interrupted Kershaw and glancing at Kieran, 'I'd be grateful if you'd leave us to continue our interrogation; otherwise, we'll take Miss Bushell back to the station.'

'Why are the police here? What's happened?' asked Fritz as Kieran grabbed his arm and pulled him out of the room.

'Marina is the illegitimate daughter of Ralph McGuire. Although very ill with Alzheimer's, Ralph died unexpectedly, and the police are investigating the circumstances surrounding his death.'

22

A few minutes had elapsed while, deep in thought, Fritz watched Kieran add milk to the coffee he had just made and then suddenly he asked, 'Why is the inspector questioning Marina?'

'Because she was the last person to see Ralph McGuire alive.'

'How did he die? Was he shot, suffocated or strangled?'

Kieran stared at Fritz, amazed, and then said, 'It was an overdose, but it was impossible for Ralph to reach the bathroom and take the tablets himself.'

'Under those circumstances, Marina shouldn't answer any more questions unless there's a solicitor present. No doubt the inspector will arrange this but I would prefer to, and I'm willing to pay for a good one. I can afford it.'

'Why should you do that?' Kieran stopped abruptly and then noticed the black dress which was spilling out of a smart carrier. Setting down his mug, Kieran reached for this whereupon the dress – slinky and with narrow straps – high-heeled sandals and flimsy lingerie all slid onto the table. Kieran stared at the garments a moment longer and then glared across the table at Fritz. 'You obviously bought this for Marina. She certainly couldn't afford it, which means you and she…'

'Steady on, she and I go…' and as Kieran moved round the table towards him, Fritz also put his mug down and held up his hands as if in protest. 'All right, hit me if you like. You obviously think I deserve it, but that's not going to help Marina.'

'Arrogant bastard! Rich, arrogant German bastard!' Kieran reached for and picked up his coffee, and after a mouthful, still staring, he asked, 'Who the hell are you anyway? Why are you here and why are you prepared to go to all that expense for Marina?'

'I'm Fritz Hauser,' and with a smile that usually charmed his female guests, 'I met Marina again yesterday. The first time for many years. As I've just said, I knew Marina years ago, when she was a courier. She used to stay at my parents' hotel near the lake with a group of holiday-makers. She was even more attractive then and I fell in love with her. I was angry and disappointed that the contract with the company wasn't renewed and although I wrote to her, Marina never replied. Then yesterday when I met her again, it was as though those years had never happened.'

'So you spent the night together?' demanded Kieran and still glaring at Fritz, 'my God! How could

I have been so dense? All that nonsense about a girls' night out when she was planning to spend it with you.'

Fritz looked at Kieran and shook his head. 'I don't know what you are talking about.'

'Marina has been very dissatisfied lately and, judging from your smart appearance and affluent manner, I'm sure she enjoyed everything you gave her.

'That dress obviously wasn't cheap, and you probably had the best suite wherever you stayed, cham–'

'Can we talk about Marina and the reason for the police being here?' interrupted Fritz. 'I gather Marina had only just met her father. Why would she give him an overdose?'

'I don't know what happened during that visit. The first I knew about Ralph McGuire being her father was on Sunday afternoon. After telling me that she was his illegitimate daughter, Marina was adamant that she would fight for whatever was due to her.'

'I still don't understand why the police are here. Why are they questioning her?'

'Marina was the last person to see Ralph McGuire alive,' repeated Kieran.

Meanwhile, Inspector Kershaw gave Marina his full attention. 'Before we were interrupted, you were telling us that Ralph couldn't speak but he understood that you were his daughter.'

Marina nodded and Kershaw continued. 'Did he indicate that you should remove your coat, that he wanted a drink?'

It was then that Marina's composure snapped. 'There was so much I wanted to tell him. That he had ignored my mother; he could have made our lives so much easier. We could have enjoyed pretty clothes, holidays.' Again, Kershaw was aware of the avarice in her voice then shook his head as she said, 'He knew my mother before Isabel.'

'That's not true. Isabel and Elspeth became friends while attending Redmaids School and Isabel often came to the house at Clifton.'

But Marina ignored this and continued. 'Why should Isabel have everything?'

'Is that why you poisoned her?' and ignoring Marina's frosty expression, 'You were seen taking something from the laburnum tree at the bottom of the Baumgartens' garden. You knew only too well that it was a laburnum tree; your grandfather had one in his garden.'

'How dare you bring him into it! He was a lovable, kind-hearted man who really loved me.'

'He was also a very clever person who imparted a lot of his horticultural knowledge. Your grandparents must have been very sad to sell their large house and garden.'

Kershaw watched as Marina's face contorted with anger. 'I was their only grandchild. That should have been mine.'

'And then you tried to push Duncan off the pavement into the traffic because you were afraid Isabel might leave the bulk of her inheritance to him.'

'He doesn't need any more. He's a successful author in his own right.' Marina's lip curled with contempt. 'He really annoyed me that evening, watching her all the time as though she was porcelain.'

Kershaw persevered: 'It all started when you visited your father.'

'I'm sure everything would have been different if he hadn't been so ill. We could have had a father and daughter relationship and he would have changed his will in my favour. I could see he was frustrated that he couldn't communicate.'

Marina paused as Fritz appeared in the doorway, still holding his mug of coffee, and looking at the inspector he said, 'Surely this has gone on long enough. We couldn't help hearing what was being said. I would suggest no more questions until a solicitor is present; and Kieran, who should return to work, agrees with me.'

Marina glared at Fritz. 'Trust you, a hotelier, to think that work is more important than me.'

'That's not true but my job is very necessary,' said Kieran, who stood behind Fritz.

Again, Marina's composure snapped. 'But what about me? You can't leave me here like this.'

Kieran turned to Kershaw. 'Is there anything I can do? Any way in which I can help?'

'No thank you, Mr O'Brien. I know where you are if I need to contact you. I'm going to take Miss Bushell back to the station for further questioning,' and ignoring Marina's 'Surely you've asked enough questions?', Kershaw persisted, 'in the presence of a solicitor.'

'I'll be responsible for his fees and any other expenses that are incurred,' said Fritz but Marina ignored this. 'It's no good asking Mr Hoskins – he's useless.' she said.

Sometime later, Inspector Kershaw watched as Marina fidgeted in her chair and asked impatiently, 'How much longer is this going to take? I've answered all these questions before. I thought I would be back at work by now.'

Marina scowled as Kershaw reminded her that this time it was for Mr Pritchard's benefit. Nothing she had said when still at Henleaze or now, before his arrival, would be admissible as evidence. The middle-aged solicitor had arrived at the station fifteen minutes after receiving Tom's phone call and had been quickly advised of the situation.

Kershaw resumed, 'However, we'll arrange for some coffee and take a break.'

'Wasting more time,' muttered Marina as Kershaw left the room, and Tom, after stating that the inspector had left the room, switched off the tape.

'Why is this taking so long, so repetitive?' asked Marina, turning to look at Mr Pritchard.

'You were the last person to see Mr McGuire, your father, alive.' The solicitor glanced up as the door opened.

A uniformed PC placed a tray of coffee on the table, the inspector returned and resumed, 'You were also wearing garments that didn't belong to you, in other words, a disguise. We've all heard that, in addition to this, a paper handkerchief in which miniscule grains of Ralph's medication were embedded, was found in the right-hand pocket. We also know that the owner of the coat never uses paper handkerch… It's all incriminating evidence. However, shall we continue?'

Mr Pritchard nodded. Marina muttered, 'Let's get on with it.' Tom switched on the tape and passed cups of coffee around.

Kershaw was aware of Marina's mutinous expression but persisted. 'I realise we've asked and you have answered these questions, but Mr Pritchard wasn't present at the time. Ralph McGuire indicated that he wanted a drink, which you gave him, ensuring that he swallowed the entire contents. We know that you returned to the bathroom to wash the glass.'

Kershaw did not refer to the two pillows which had been on the floor, beside the bed, or that Ralph had been lying flat on his back when Isabel returned, and asked, 'Was your father still leaning against his pillows when you came out of the bathroom and, soon after that, left the room?'

'Yes, but I've already told you that,' retorted Marina as she brushed aside Mr Pritchard's restraining hand and ignored his comment: 'You must have been very upset at seeing your father so ill.'

'I'm quite sure Marina is capable of saying that herself,' commented Kershaw.

'What would you have done if it had been your father?' Marina glared defiantly at the inspector. Then, under her breath, she muttered, 'In any case, he owed me.'

Marina's words, which were not as inaudible as she intended, reached Kershaw, whose gaze met Pritchard's agonised expression and, aware of Tom sitting beside him, still and expectant, the inspector intoned, 'Marina Bushell, I hereby charge you with the murder of your father, Ralph McGuire.'

Marina's hiss of disapproval smothered Kershaw's inaudible conclusion: 'But what was your motive – MERCY or MERCENARY?'